*A
Harlequin
Romance*

OTHER

Harlequin Romances

by MARY WIBBERLEY

THE
WILDERNESS HUT

by

MARY WIBBERLEY

Harlequin Books

TORONTO • LONDON • NEW YORK • AMSTERDAM • SYDNEY • WINNIPEG

Original hard cover edition published in 1975
by Mills & Boon Limited

SBN 373-01968-8

Harlequin edition published April 1976

Printed in Canada

CHAPTER ONE

EVE CARRICK stood at the bedroom window and watched the man standing on the lawn in the glow of the setting sun. He was talking to her host. Neither of them could see her, for she had paused in the act of switching the light on, and had then gone, curious, to the window.

He was tall and broadly built. His face – was it handsome or not? Not conventionally so, *certainly*, but it could have been, years ago, before he'd had – what? a fight? Rugged, slightly battered features as if he had broken his nose at one time and not bothered to do anything about it. He had a wide stubborn mouth and chin – where *had* they found him, for heaven's sake? Crooked eyebrows that were thick but not too much so – they went with the dark eyes that were thickly lashed. A thin scar ran down his right cheek, only two or three inches long – but she would not have been surprised if it turned out to be a slash from a duelling sword, because he looked out of his time somehow. Regarding him as she was from her hidden viewing point, Eve thought: you should have been here in the eighteenth century, you'd have been more at home then. One thing was sure – she knew that she would not like him.

She turned away from the window. Esko and Liisa would be wondering where she had got to. Already the

5

two men were coming towards the house, and she had a memory of that first glimpse of the stranger – the man who would be guide on her journey – and the navy blue Beatle type hat he wore at a rakish angle seemed to set the seal on the type of man he would be. Casual, uncaring – but more. Eve had seen what could be a hard ruthlessness in those last few seconds. She paused as she picked up her handbag, the reason for her visit to her room in the first place. It was what she wanted, of course; she needed a guide, a pilot to take her to a remote part of Finland, someone who knew the way and could be relied upon. Esko had assured her that Garth Seton was just such a man. And now she was going to meet him. Eve passed the long wardrobe mirror on her way to the door, and paused. The room was shadowy now, but she didn't bother to switch the light on to check her appearance. She knew she looked good because she never looked otherwise, she knew she was beautiful because she had been assured so by everyone she had ever met, and she had the time and the money to ensure that that state of affairs would last. At nineteen, Eve was the ideal of what every teenager would like to be – and she knew it. She smiled at her reflection and saw the shadowy, blurred image smiling back at her. Then she walked on towards the door, along the broad corridor, and down the stairs.

They were talking, the three of them, Esko and Liisa Virtanen and Garth Seton, in the brightly lit living room of the house, and Liisa turned first, seeing Eve, and broke away from the little group and came towards her.

6

"Here you are," she said, and her plump face was smiling, as always. "Garth has arrived." She put her hand on Eve's arm, as if to draw her towards the others. He turned then, turned and looked at Eve, and there was none of the shock reaction she was so used to, the: "My God, what a beautiful face" type of wonder. Just a look that seemed to say: "So you're Eve Carrick, the wealthy Eve Carrick who dashes anywhere she pleases on the slightest whim, and has everyone jumping to attention when she cracks the whip."

And then he smiled, and she knew it had all been her imagination, and wondered what on earth was the matter with her. It was only slight, a cool polite smile and he held out his hand.

"How d'you do," he said. He had a deep pleasant voice, and she hadn't seen how tall he was from the bedroom window, but he topped her by a good six inches and she was five foot nine. He had removed the Beatle cap, of course, and the check lumberjacket he had worn, and the black sweater over blue jeans was tight enough to show he had a broad chest and powerful arms. The hair was nearly black – and so were his eyes, a dark dark grey – and hard as flint. Matching the rest of the face, she thought, about which she saw no reason to change her opinion. He *did* look out of his time, and that scar was neither less nor more sinister in the warm light of the room.

Esko looked at his wife, and gave an imperceptible jerk of the head. *"Kylla,"* she said. "Come, Esko, we will go and prepare dinner, and leave Eve and Garth to talk."

7

Esko was a typical Finn, stockily built, blond, broad face, especially the cheekbones, and he smiled now at Eve and nodded. "Good, good," he said. "You can talk, and soon we will eat." His English was better than his wife's, but then he travelled frequently to London on business with Eve's father, while Liisa stayed at home to look after their young twin daughters. He put his arm affectionately on his wife's shoulders, and Eve watched them go out, then turned to Garth.

"All right," she said. "We might as well be comfortable. Are you going to sit down?" and she moved gracefully, because that was the way she had been taught at finishing school, towards the settee and sank down into it.

"No, thanks," he said pleasantly enough. "I prefer to stand. I've been sitting for hours in the plane and it's good to stretch my legs," and he gave her that slight smile again.

So that meant that Eve had to look up at him, which annoyed her for no reason she could put a finger on. She was about to ask him where he had just flown from when he said: "Esko tells me you want me to take you to Rovaniemi and then maybe on somewhere else. Is that correct?"

"Yes." She nodded. "Are you prepared to do it?"

He shrugged. "Of course. Why not?" The shrug seemed to say that if she was mad enough to pay him to take her somewhere she could get to quite easily by scheduled air flight he didn't care. And Eve had no intention of doing any explaining to *him*.

"And Esko has agreed the price with you?"

8

"Yes. It's a lot of money for a young girl like you to be flinging about, isn't it?"

She looked up sharply, stung. No one in London would have dared to speak to her like that, and it showed in her eyes. "I don't think that's any of your business," she said coldly.

" Oh, sure it's not. You're employing me. You're the boss," but the grin that accompanied the words wasn't at all chastened. "So when do you want to set off?"

"Tomorrow."

"Tomorrow it is. Do you want to see the plane now? It's on the lake."

"After dinner, perhaps." Damn you, she thought, who do you think you are, calling me a young girl, how dare you!

"After dinner will be dark – boss." The last word, so softly spoken, almost imagined, was an insult. Anger flared within Eve, swift anger, as quickly controlled. Because she had promised her father faithfully that she would go north with the man so highly recommended by Esko Virtanen and she had never broken a promise to her father yet. But she would not take sheer impertinence from him either. She rose to her feet and faced him.

"Let's get one thing clear from the start, Mr. Seton," she said, with a sweet smile masking the cold anger. "You do not call me boss. Eve or Miss Carrick will do, but I don't like cheek from an employee."

"Forgive me," he laid his hand across his chest, "Eve." He made the word almost a caress. "It was a slip of the tongue, for which I crave your pardon. You will, of course, as my employer, call me Garth, I trust?"

"If you like." She turned away, and towards the window. The lake could only be dimly seen from the house, but there was a gleam of white, a bobbing and a movement on the water. "What kind of plane is it?"

"A Cessna floatplane. I have to land on water – but that's no problem in a country like this." He had followed her to the window, and she saw the dark reflection mirrored in the glass, slightly blurred at the edges because of the double glazing, but he was big and powerful, that image was clear enough. She didn't turn round. She didn't particularly want to look at him because something about his expression was disturbing to her.

"What is your job exactly, Garth?" she said. "Or shouldn't I ask?"

"I ferry people about," he answered. "I take them to where they want to go – or I take cargo."

"I see." Eve turned then, turned to face him. "You know I'll want you for about two weeks? Going up to Rovaniemi, waiting and then returning?"

"Yes. I know. Esko told me." But there was something in those flint grey eyes, some hidden light she could not define. Surely not – amusement? Why should he be amused? "He says you're going to visit an old friend – but she doesn't know you're coming. Is that right?"

Was that why he was amused? "I do lots of things on impulse," she answered calmly. "And why not? I can afford to," and she smiled. Let him see if he had a retort to that. "It will be a surprise for her."

"And if she's moved, gone away, and you can't find her, it'll be a surprise for *you*," he remarked.

"So?" she shrugged. "It will be a trip – a holiday if you like. And work for you. Why should you complain?"

"I'm not complaining," one of the thick dark eyebrows lifted fractionally. "I'm merely wondering, that's all. Wondering what makes people like you tick."

"Maybe you'll find out, won't you?" Eve answered, pleasantly enough, and moved away from him. "I'll see the plane when we leave. Esko recommended you, and I'll take his word that you– and your plane – are as reliable as he says. I'm too tired to see it now. I only arrived in Helsinki today from London."

"Ah yes, dear old London. How is it?"

She glanced sharply at him. Was there mockery in his every word, or was it her imagination? Everything he said, every fleeting expression on his face, were underlaid with something – something, but what on earth was it? She was confident, poised, completely and utterly self-assured, and yet Eve found herself puzzled and faintly – there was only one word for it – faintly *disturbed* by this man.

Later that night, when the house was quiet and still, Eve lay in bed and let her mind roam over the evening. There had been nothing she could fault with Garth Seton. His behaviour throughout the dinner and afterwards had been perfectly correct; his manners easy and polished, and when their hosts' two eight-year-old twin daughters had come back home from the

11

friends' house, where they had been to a party, he had been affably friendly to them, speaking in fluent Finnish because their English was as yet limited, making them laugh, and Eve had watched their faces light up, had seen the way he so clearly charmed them. But he doesn't charm me, she thought, as she lay on her back looking at the faint light on the ceiling from a chink in the curtains. He doesn't charm me at all. And that was odd – but she knew why; it was because he wasn't even trying. And no one had ever *not* tried before. No man, that was. From an early age Eve had been used to adoration and adulation from every male she had encountered. She accepted it as her due, just as easily as she accepted the money that her father had poured into her lap – metaphorically speaking – ever since she had been old enough to want things. At first toys, then, later, clothes, jewellery, furs – cars. At nineteen Eve owned a superb sports car that was the envy of her friends. She thought about that, thought about her friends as her mind turned full circle and reached again the reason for her being here in Finland.

My friends, she mouthed softly into the cool darkness. I wonder where you all are, what you are all doing now. Whooping it up at a party? Dining, dancing – what? And I wonder if you're missing me? But she knew the answer to that one already and faint tears pricked the backs of her eyes. It was why she had come away, she knew that too, why she had felt that restless urge to travel that overcame her every so often when she just had to get away from the mad helter-skelter whirl of the life she led. Because how did she ever know

12

whether her friends were her friends because of herself – or because of the money, the prestige – *the fact that she was William Carrick's – the William Carrick of Carrick Papers – daughter?* She didn't. She never would know. Her mind went back to supper the previous night. Just her and her father, by the fire in their gracious Hampstead home, and William Carrick had looked at Eve and said:

"Sure you want to go, love?"

"Quite sure. It'll be a change, if nothing else." And Eve had looked at her father, and seen the lines on his face, lines of strain that nothing could erase. "Why don't you come with me?" she had added, on a sudden impulse she herself didn't understand.

For a moment he had smiled. "That's the first time you've ever said that," he remarked. "I wonder why?"

"You look as though you need a rest. You look – tired."

"I'll be all right," William Carrick shook his head faintly. "I've had – it's just that I've had a lot on my mind lately. But if you change your mind, decide not to go –" and he stopped.

Thinking back, now, Eve realized she had been puzzled at the time by his words, by the *way* he said them. It was almost as if he wanted her to change her mind and not go to Finland. But why? He had never stopped her going anywhere previously. And his strange request, weeks before, when she had first decided to go on impulse to see Heli, that she should humour him by letting Esko pick a reliable man to escort her into the "wilds of Lapland" as he had put it,

13

that too had puzzled her. But she had agreed, more in amusement than anything else.

Heli. Heli Salko. The one true friend she had ever had. Long flaxen-haired Heli, with whom Eve could be herself, because no amount of money would impress the quiet-faced Finnish girl who had been so lonely at first at Eve's school, until Eve had taken her under her wing and looked after her. Six years ago it had been, and they had kept in touch when Heli had gone back to Finland, her father's two-year stint in the Embassy finished, had kept in touch until a year ago, when Eve, caught up in a busy social whirl, had somehow found letters more difficult to write . . .

It was her own fault, she knew that. She had changed immeasurably in the past two years, and things which had once seemed important faded in the glow of new, brighter friendships. A glow that occasionally became tinselly and false . . . Eve sighed. In a way, this journey was a journey to the past. And perhaps, just perhaps, she would be able to recapture something of that careless happiness she had known in the days of her friendship with Heli. Maybe. Strange how the idea had come, weeks ago. On one of her rare evenings alone with her father, he had recalled her younger schooldays, had wondered what had happened to Heli . . . It had triggered off the idea, and ideas, once triggered off with Eve, had a habit of coming rapidly to fruition. And here she was, and tomorrow she would set off in a plane with a strange, dark, somehow forbidding character called Garth, to surprise her friend Heli. The last letter she had sent several weeks previously had not been answered, and Heli was always prompt – or had been. Perhaps she had moved. Eve turned and prepared to settle down for sleep. She would soon know. How surprised Heli would be!

Esko and Liisa were up early the following morning, Friday. Eve heard their movements from downstairs as she lay, in the first waking moments, cocooned in the warmth of the soft mattress on which she had slept. She must have been tired, for she had no recollection of falling asleep, only vague memories of her thoughts in bed, thoughts about her father, about Heli – about Garth. She could hardly ask her hosts how they had come to know a man like that. It would be an impertinence. Yet she was curious, intensely so, and that was annoying, for Eve considered it a weakness to be so interested in another person – one moreover that she didn't particularly like.

She lay there, loath to move, knowing she must soon, and yet it was so warm, so very warm, and comfortable . . .

"Eve? Are you awake?" A man's voice, from outside the door, a quick rapping of the knuckles. The voice was not Esko's. Garth? *Garth?*

"Yes?" she answered.

"Can I come in?"

"Yes." It was Garth. Dressed in jeans, warm grey sweater under denim jacket. Garth – carrying a cup of coffee. Eve took a deep breath.

"Good morning. Our hosts are busy getting the children ready for school, so I volunteered." He

15

grinned crookedly at her and sat on the edge of the bed. "I thought it was the least I could do."

"It's very kind of you." She took the cup and saucer from him. "Thank you." And then she waited. He didn't stand up, merely looked at her, and she saw, not for the first time, but it hadn't really registered before, that his eyes were very cool and watchful. The sort of eyes that take it all in. Very useful for a pilot, thought Eve dryly, but a touch annoying when you're sitting up in bed clad only in a blue nylon nightie.

"Don't let me detain you," she said, as pleasantly as she could.

"Oh, you're not," he looked faintly surprised. "I thought you might want to ask me something – you know, details of the journey – or even brief me on it. I mean, have you any definite instructions for me?" It seemed impossible, but there was that constant edge in his voice, almost imperceptible, but *there* – hard amusement. He was impossible!

"I'm leaving it to you," she answered. "You've been so highly recommended by Esko that I wouldn't have thought you would feel it necessary to ask *me* anything. As long as you get me to Rovaniemi today – and then we'll take it from there – you'll be doing the job I hired you to do."

"As you say." He nodded. The scar looked faintly more sinister in the curtained half light of her bedroom. His eyes were shadowed too, so that they might have been black, not grey, but there was no mistaking the whiteness of his teeth as he smiled suddenly. "Then I'll go. And let you get dressed. Breakfast will be ready in

16

about fifteen minutes, Liisa asked me to say." He stood up, half turned, paused and then turned back to Eve. He put his finger up and stroked the scar on his cheek, just gently. "It was a broken bottle. Nothing so romantic as a knife, I'm afraid."

And Eve felt herself do something she had not done for a long time. She blushed. "What on earth do you mean?"

"You were curious, weren't you? Oh, come on, don't give me that cool 'touch-me-not' look of yours. You've been looking at it often enough – I thought I'd satisfy your curiosity. See you later." And he went out. Eve took a few deep breaths to calm herself. The sheer damned *impertinence* of the man! "You've been looking at it often enough –" and worse: "Don't give me that cool 'touch-me-not' look–"

"Oh!" she glared at the closed door. Swallowing the last of the hot sweet coffee, as if it might calm her, Eve let the significance of his taunt sink fully in. In just a few brief words quickly and quietly spoken, he had described how she knew a lot of people found her. *She* knew, deep down, but no one ever dared to say – except him. "Touch-me-not," she repeated softly. That is how I am, and I can't help it. I don't let anyone get too close, not even my friends, because that is the way I am. The thoughts filled her mind, and would not go away. Slowly, because they had the power to hurt, she got out of bed. It was time to get up, not time for self-analysis. I don't need that, she thought fiercely. And especially, I don't need someone like *you*, who I am employing, to speak to me like some head-shrinker.

17

But as she sat by the mirror making up, Eve paused and looked, really looked at herself. Her dark honey-gold hair was in a loose casual style, reaching to shoulder length. It was the way she preferred to wear it. She had several wigs and hair-pieces for evening wear, expensive ones, matching her own rich honey tresses exactly, and undetectable in wear. Her eyebrows and lashes were naturally darker, and she twirled the brush and applied a touch more mascara to enhance their lustre. She looked down at the array of exotic jars and bottles before her, the very minimum with which she would travel, and then back again to the glass. Her eyes were a clear tawny gold, harmonising with her hair, her face a perfect oval, small fine nose, full soft lips.

She saw it all, and knew the satisfaction of being simply beautiful – and the mocking image of Garth's face swam mistily into view for one second, and some of the satisfaction vanished. Strange, for his opinion was not of the slightest importance, but so. The taunt still stung. Touch-me-not. And the look in his eyes said more than that for him. It said: You may think you're beautiful, but you're not to *me*. Coolly, deliberately, Eve applied a touch more lipstick, her favourite shade, a frosty pink that emphasised the delicacy of her face, and then she flicked the comb through her hair, and pulled a small face at the mirror. "Beast!" she mouthed, and the reflection caught the word, and bounced it back. Standing, Eve swept her array of bottles and jars into her beauty bag and placed it on top of her packed suitcases. She smoothed down the

18

slim-fitting white sweater over her hips, checked that her black and white checked trousers were just so, and, picking up her huge black handbag, went down to breakfast.

CHAPTER TWO

As they skimmed the surface of the lake, she turned back to wave to Esko and Liisa, standing there, the sun catching their upturned faces, the trees behind them partially hiding their house and smaller sauna house which stood a few yards away from it. The picture they made was sharp, clear, and colourful. Because the air was so clean and fresh, everything was etched in brilliance. The brightness of the grass, the shimmering waters of the lake, Esko and Liisa's own clothes, and behind them the tall wooden house, so cosy and secure. Secure in love, thought Eve as she turned at last away, for that was abundantly clear. It was there in the atmosphere of the house, in everything about the place, that her hosts were content with each other, with their two daughters, and with their life. And it was as if Garth caught something of this, for even though he was concentrating on the controls as he lifted the small plane from the water and away, now skimming the tree tops, he said: "They seem to be very happy people, don't they?"

"Yes." But his words puzzled her. For were they not old friends? "Don't you know them very well?"

"As well as I know anyone in this life," and he laughed. "But things aren't always what they seem, are they?"

She didn't answer. For the first time since considering this trip to Finland, a small edge of doubt touched Eve, and there was a coldness within her. I'm a fool, she thought. Dashing recklessly off into the blue again, just because it seemed a good idea, and now sitting in this tiny plane with a stranger I don't know, don't like, and am beginning to wonder if I trust. She closed her eyes. I know what Esko and Liisa think about me, she thought in sudden awareness. They think I'm rich and spoilt and can go anywhere in the world that I want, any time I want – only they're too polite to say so, and Esko deals with my father, so will do anything to help me. What they don't know, she thought, is that doing all this jazzing about doesn't make me a happy person. What does? But she didn't know the answer to that one.

"Don't tell me you're falling asleep," the dry voice brought her out of her introspection. The voice that had the power already, on such a brief acquaintance, of making Eve's hackles rise. And she definitely didn't know why *that* should be so. But it was. This man – who was working for her for the next week at least – was a tough individual who managed to hide any gentler side to his nature very successfully, had a hard edge of amusement in his tones when speaking to her, and, most irksome of all, appeared totally immune to her. She took her time answering.

"I was thinking," she said. "And even if I had been falling asleep, which I wasn't, your question would certainly have woken me, wouldn't it?"

"Mmm, yes, you have a point there," and he turned and grinned at her suddenly. "Still, I was only going to suggest – tentatively, of course, because I'd hate to

21

appear to be telling *you* what to do – that if you were tired you could lie down on that reclining seat behind us. That's all." His face now reflected bland, helpful innocence.

Eve looked round. "Thanks," she said. "But I'll stay here. We should be in Rovaniemi soon, shouldn't we?"

"In a few hours. This little bus isn't as fast as your Finnair, you know, but it does me nicely. Any time you want to stop, tell me, we can always put down on a lake, in which, you will have noted, this country abounds. Give me enough notice and I'll stop on a lake that has a café near. But I've brought a flask that Liisa filled with coffee for me if you need a drink."

"Thank you." What had he been doing, she suddenly wondered, to get a broken bottle pushed into his face? Brawling in a pub, or night club? But she was not going to ask, and didn't even know why that thought should have come to her out of the blue. "Shall I pour you a cup?"

"Yes, you can do."

She took her time, careful to unscrew the top of the flask so that none spilled out. The movement of the plane was smooth enough, not as comfortable as a jet, of course, but certainly in no way unpleasant. And whatever his other faults and failings, Eve had an instinctive trust of his abilities as a pilot. Those hard level eyes, the hands so steady on the joystick, all inspired confidence in her. Not that she was apprehensive. She enjoyed flying, and had never been nervous either in a plane, or in any other form of travel.

Passing him the cup of steaming coffee was easy

enough, but the tingle that touched her fingers when their hands unavoidably made brief contact was disconcerting. She surreptitiously rubbed her hand down her side as if that would dispel the treacherous sensation. And she made sure, when he handed the empty cup back to her, that it didn't happen again.

"Thanks. Mind if I smoke?"

"Of course not."

"Do you?"

"Do I what? Smoke?"

"Yes."

"No."

"Oh!"

What a stupid conversation, she thought. But at least it's preferable to the sharp-edged antagonism that seems to creep in most of the time we talk. In a way it was a challenge. I wonder, she thought suddenly, if we could speak without arguing? And turning to him, smiling, she said, as she watched him light a thin black cheroot: "This is the most breathtaking scenery, isn't it? It must be wonderful to live here." The forest and glittering lakes spread out on all sides below and around them, dark rich pines, gaunt spruces, and everywhere that wasn't covered in trees was water, still and cool, catching the sun and so calm and tranquil that Eve wished that she could be part of it all, instead of what she was. And that brief thought, swiftly as it passed, disturbed and troubled her. What a strange notion to have!

"It certainly is," he agreed. "But it's a tough country as well. It's cold and hard in winter.

Temperatures well below-zero – especially the further north you get, and hardly any daytime to speak of. It wouldn't do you at all."

She took a deep breath. Perhaps it *was* impossible after all. "Meaning that I'm soft?" she asked quietly.

He spared her a glance. Blue smoke wreathed the cabin, the scent tangy and exotic. "No offence, but look at you."

"I have, frequently," she retorted. "I've got two arms and legs, the same as anyone else. So?"

That swift amused grin, slightly crooked, the dark grey eyes narrowed in amusement – and that laugh. "So, you need something else to survive in these parts. There's a word in Finnish: *sisu*, that perfectly describes their own character – a mixture of hardiness, perseverance, stamina – and a touch of stubbornness. That's what *they* have, and what anyone who decides to make their home here must have. It's fine to come here for a holiday – a lot of them speak English, so you don't even need to make the effort at understanding a strange tongue –" that was a finely barbed insult, and Eve's fingers tightened on her bag, "– and I dare say you have a touch of stubbornness, but the other qualities –" he pursed his lips and shook his head slowly.

"Do you practise being rude, or does it come naturally to you?" she asked.

His laughter filled the plane. "Ouch! I felt the icicles then. *Touché*. Was I being so very rude? And you my employer too. I'll shut up and let you do all the talking, how about that?"

"I doubt if you could," she answered dryly.

"True," he conceded. "But I'll be more careful what I say. You know — watch every word and count ten before I speak. How would that suit you?"

"Just tell me why you feel the need to insult me, that's all," she answered.

"Do you really want to know? Not why I feel the need — as you put it — to insult you, because I wasn't aware of doing so — but do you want to know why I speak as I do?"

She wasn't sure, all of a sudden, if she did, but it was too late to back down now. "Yes," she said.

"Then I'll tell you. I don't like people who have money throwing their weight around. And you may not have been aware of it at Esko and Liisa's, but that was precisely what you were doing. Oh, I don't mean in any *obvious* way, but it was there all the time, the air of knowing that you were *you*, the important Miss Eve Carrick, and they'd better jump to it — or else —"

"How can you —" she began.

"Let me finish." His voice, harder than hers, stopped her in mid-sentence. "I'll bet you're not used to hearing the truth about yourself, are you? Wealthy people are well cushioned against all the nastiness of life. Well, you can tell me to stop any time you choose, if that's what you prefer, but if you want my opinions, at least hear them out. Okay?"

"Go on," she said, her voice very taut.

He glanced across at her. Eve sat very still, waiting. In a strange way, his words were neither less nor more than she expected. There was an odd sensation within

25

her, as if she had been expecting something like this to happen for a long time. And now it was, and it was almost with a feeling of relief that she listened to his words. As if she *had* to hear them.

"That's the gist of it. I've seen you with them, as a guest in their house, eating their food – and I saw Liisa's face as she watched you. She was frightened that if everything wasn't just so, you might tell your father and he'd be cross – and Esko would suffer. Do you know what time she was up this morning, preparing breakfast, making sure everything was just perfect? Six o'clock. While you slumbered peacefully on. That's why I brought you coffee in bed. *She* was going to bring you your breakfast up, because she thought you might be used to it, but I told her I'd take your coffee up and ask you, and when I got down I told her you'd be coming down to eat."

"If Liisa's so frightened of displeasing me – *if* – aren't you scared that I'll tell my father that *you're* grossly impertinent, and as they recommended you, they'll still be in trouble?" she asked. She hid the shock well, as she did any deep emotion. She was able to speak quite calmly and rationally. At least he wouldn't know.

"I've not been grossly impertinent. I've spoken the truth, whether you like it or not. But I'll tell you something. If you did say anything, and Esko landed in trouble, *you* would regret it, I promise you that." And he gave her a cool, cool look. A cold shiver of fear touched Eve's spine. There is something far more frightening about words softly spoken than in shouted threats.

"You were glad enough to take my money," she said at last. "Is this how you treat your employers?"

"I decided to fly you as a favour to them," he answered softly. "That's all. Your money doesn't impress me, believe me. I have sufficient for my needs, and that's all that anyone wants, if you think about it."

"Rubbish!" she answered, her voice sharp. "Everyone wants more. If everyone had your attitude, the world would grind to a halt."

"Would it? Is it doing so marvellously well now? And in any case, I'm not trying to force my opinions on others, merely stating them. Perhaps I can help create a balance, who knows?" And he shrugged.

"Will you stop, please?" asked Eve. "When you see a suitable place, that is. I'd like a coffee and something to eat."

"All right. Keep your eyes open." The subject was changed, but the atmosphere had not. They flew on in silence for about fifteen minutes or so, then Garth said: "Fasten your seat belt, I can see a café."

A swift descent, a soft feather landing on the lake, and they skimmed along leaving a flurry of spray in their wake as Garth manoeuvred the plane to the very water's edge. A silence after the engine put-puttered out, and Eve looked at him.

"Have you anything more to say, any more *opinions*, before we get out?" she asked. "Because if so, please tell me now. I'd like to enjoy my coffee."

"I think I've said enough for one morning," he answered. "We'll talk about the weather, the latest films – anything you like in future." His face *was* hard,

27

there was no getting away from that, and she had never seen eyes like his on any man. There was strength and stubbornness there, just as there was in the rest of his face – in the rest of him, for that matter. But more, his eyes, his dark, dark grey eyes, held a depth, a knowledge to them that was disconcerting in the oddest way. It was as if he knew – everything. Yet how could he? How could he know anything of her?

"Tell me," he said, quite mildly for him, "is it the scar which fascinates you? Do you want to know the full sordid story?" And it was then that Eve realized she had been staring. A second's breath, her eyes cool and shuttered.

"Is it a sordid story?" she managed to inject an 'I'm not at all surprised' note into her words. "No, thank you. And was I staring at it? Forgive me, I do know it's rude to stare. Shall we go?"

"I'll go first. We may or may not need wellies, according to how close I've managed to get to shore. Still, don't worry, I always keep a couple of spare pairs for my passengers." And he looked at her and smiled. He's waiting for me to show shock – or disgust – at having to get out in such a primitive way, she thought, knowing. So I won't.

"That's fine," she said, and followed him to the door.

"Hmm. Better than I thought," he said. "Pity I've not got a boat, like Esko, but there's no need for you to get your dainty feet wet," and so saying he lowered himself into the clear shallows and lifted his arms. "Okay, gently now. I'll carry you."

Eve resisted the temptation to use her dainty feet in a most undainty manner and kick his teeth down his throat, took a deep breath and slid into a pair of strong arms. One deft turn about, two steps, and he deposited her on a shingly bank and grinned. "You're quite heavy for such a slim girl," he said. "It must be your bones."

"I'm nine stone – I'm sorry you're not very strong," Eve answered in her sweetest voice. The 'dainty feet' remark still rankled. "How much do *you* weigh?"

"Me?" He frowned. "I haven't bothered for ages. About fourteen stone, I think."

"Perhaps you ought to take up exercise," she answered, "to improve your stamina," and she walked away from him, pleased with her parting shot. He caught up with her as she scrambled up the grassy bank. Ahead of them, forest, thick tall trees hiding the sun, through it, several minutes walk away, a main road, several parked cars – and a café. They had circled round it before Garth landed, to get the bearings of it, so that Eve knew precisely in which direction she had to walk to get there . . .

"This way," he touched her arm and she frowned.

"No – *this* way," pointing.

He smiled a very tolerant, patient smile. "You've got a little confused, I'm afraid. The café is due west of the spot we landed and that's here –"

"Don't be ridiculous! I remember as you circled it thinking that we'd just cut through these trees and –"

"And did you allow for the curve of the lake?"

29

Eve slowed her footsteps and thought about that. "No," she admitted. "But –"

"Look, I've a compass on board. Want me to get it?"

"No. I'll follow you."

They were inside the trees now; green and shadowy light filtered through, and the twigs made a semi-soft crunchy carpet underfoot. And Garth stopped and turned and looked down at her. "Look," he said quietly, "I'm not trying to be awkward or argumentative now, but I do know a little more than you about navigation, and there was just no point in letting us both get lost to prove a point. Do you see?"

"Oh, I see all right." He was disconcertingly tall. She thought: If he kissed me now, there'd be no one to hear, no one to call – what a *terrible* thought to have! Quickly she went on: "You are my guide. I must let you guide me, mustn't I? Lead on." Without a word, he turned and went onwards, leaving her to follow. He lopes along, she thought, like a wolf padding silently through a forest after its prey. And then she remembered their conversation before, his hard comments, the harsh cruelty of them – and she knew now, now that they had had time to sink in, that they had really hurt. Because it is one thing to think you know what people are saying about you – it is quite another to hear the views expressed, forcefully, succinctly. As he had. No one had ever done anything like that to her before. She could say to him: "You're fired. I don't want *you* to take me anywhere." But that, in a way, would be cowardly. It would be running away – it would be, what was that he had said? "Wealthy people are well cushioned against all the nastiness of life." It would go to prove that what he said was right.

Eve lifted her chin up. More than ever she needed to see Heli. That sweet calmness, a sturdiness of personality that Eve had not encountered in anyone else, would help her see this man in perspective. He was nobody important. Why should she let him bother her?

"Why didn't you try and phone your friend from Helsinki? It would have saved you a journey if she's moved." His voice was an intrusion, bringing her back with a bump.

"I want it to be a surprise. Do you mind?" she rejoined tartly. Although he had a point, she resented his saying it. How could she tell him that she needed an excuse to get away from the whirl of life – and memories of Heli, and her father's remarks, had triggered off the urge. She *could* have telephoned from London, for that matter. But in a way, this was what she preferred to do. To see and talk to Heli, to spend some time with her, would be perfect. But to have a target in mind gave a valid reason for her desire to escape from her other friends for a couple of weeks. And Eve sighed. That was one thing he, Garth, wouldn't understand in a million years. No doubt he had his impressions of the jet set from the newspapers and gossip magazines. The gay heady champagne life – of which Eve was a part. She couldn't see him fitting into it, not in any way.

As he walked ahead, and the trees thinned, Eve had a mental picture of him beside two of her current male admirers, John and Neil. Polo-playing, hunting, yachting – their lives were full. They were witty, both of them in their separate ways, had plenty of money, travelled as they chose, and had both been educated at the "in" places, John at Eton, Neil at Harrow. And this man – who was he? And yet – and yet – suddenly, and to her great surprise, Eve saw the image of him quite clearly with them – and knew something that was a shock to her. He would not be out of place. For all his casual clothes, and even more casual manners, there was nothing gauche or self-conscious about him. He was all man, not only tough and strong, but as assured as anyone she knew. The question repeated itself in her brain. *Who* was he? Who on earth was he?

CHAPTER THREE

SHE was tired when they reached Rovaniemi. Not just the fatigue of travel, but that of knowing she had in a way been analysed by the man who was even now circling a lake on the outskirts of the town preparatory to landing. After their short stay at the café by the roadside, Eve had gone to the ladies' room to wash, and he had vanished in the direction of the garage connecting, to emerge with a cardboard box from the store next to it.

"Provisions," he told her, as if she had been about to ask, which was rather annoying, because, although curious, she had decided she would not give him that satisfaction.

"Why, do you think we'll be hungry before Rovaniemi? I won't, I assure you."

He laughed. "Not you. I always keep a good supply of tinned food aboard. Just in case." They began walking back to the lake. The last three words hung in the air quite unbearably, until Eve could stand it no longer.

"Just in case of what?"

He shrugged. "In case I have to make a landing miles away from anywhere."

"Is it likely?" They walked side by side now, Eve having to stride out to match his longer steps, and she didn't really care if he did have to land miles away from anywhere, just as long as *she* wasn't with him, but making polite conversation was a lot easier than letting him tear her verbally apart.

"Highly unlikely, actually. But sometimes I set off – when I've got a few days free – find a quiet lake and an *autiotupa* and have me a pleasant rest, and some fishing."

"I see. And who or what is an *autiotupa*?"

"I'm glad you asked that. It's a what, not a who. It's a deserted hut, or more precisely, a wilderness hut. There are hundreds of them dotted around Finland and Lapland. They're quite free, anyone can stay, and the only rules are to leave them as you find them."

"How fascinating," Eve murmured.

"By which you mean – how ghastly. Your tone doesn't fool me."

"It wouldn't pay for us all to have the same tastes, would it?" she answered, remembering something he had said.

He gave her one of those hard level looks which said a lot – none of it flattering. "You're so right. It wouldn't. I can't imagine anything less tranquil than hordes of noisy tourists tramping through the forests from shelter to shelter. Finland has an atmosphere of its own. It's a different place from the rest of Europe, even the rest of Scandinavia. Let's try and keep it that way."

"Is that why you live here?" she said.

"Partly."

"Because you don't like the rest of Europe?"

"Not necessarily. I didn't say that. But I have ties

34

here –" and he stopped. "But you're not interested in me. Come, we're nearly there."

Ties? What kind? Eve wouldn't ask. To do so would be to risk a rebuff, and she didn't want that.

She thought about that as he skimmed along the water at Rovaniemi. Since entering the plane again they had spoken comparatively few words, which had given Eve time to think about a lot of things . . .

"Okay. Shall we find some place to eat first – or do you want to go and see if your friend is at her address?"

The lake on which they had landed was clearly on the outskirts of the town. She could see houses, a church, white and gleaming in sunlight, roads – and cars. And people. But nobody thought it strange to see a floatplane on their lake. Perhaps they were used to them. Only a child, walking past with its mother, gave them a second glance, and then was gone.

Eve looked blankly at him, her mind still full of a jumble of colourful impressions. Reindeer wandering loose in fields in much the same way as cows would in England . . . The red pantiled roofs of the houses in Rovaniemi as they circled lower and lower, looking for a place to land. . . A white tall, spired church with grey-green roof just a few minutes back, large, imposing, beautiful, and, a few miles after they had had coffee, a bear, partially hidden by trees, but Garth had pointed, told her to look, and she had seen the huge shambling creature just before it vanished into the pines, perhaps frightened by the noise of their engine. And now, at last, she was here – a mere couple of miles from the Arctic Circle. Eve had travelled widely, when and where she chose, but there was some atmosphere, something inexplicable here that she had never experienced before . . .

"Sorry?" she said.

He repeated his question. "Do you want to eat?"

"Are you hungry?" she asked him.

"In a word – yes," he answered.

"Then we'll eat, of course."

"Aren't you hungry?" he asked, as if he didn't really care anyway but felt the need to attempt a show of manners.

"Not really, but I suppose I should. Do you know a place?"

"Yes. Near here. And while we're there we'll ask where your friend's address is. You do have it on you, I suppose?"

She touched her bag lightly. "Yes."

"Then we'll go." He still wore the wellingtons, his jeans tucked into them. And that ridiculous hat. He looked like a fisherman. She wondered what sort of place he could possibly be taking her to, and shuddered slightly. If it was at all rough she would just refuse to go in. Let him. She would find somewhere. She had a Finnish and Swedish phrase book tucked in her handbag. I'll manage, she thought. But her phrase book was not needed. The restaurant to which he took her was a large modern building, all windows and light, exceptionally clean-looking, and within a short walk of their lake, which prompted her to ask, as he opened the door for her to go in: "Do you know this town well?"

"Reasonably so. I've been here before, if that's what you mean, and the food's good."

It wasn't quite what she had meant, but she decided to leave the subject. The restaurant was nearly empty. A few couples and families dotted the room, a few more people wandered round a large loaded table, plates in hands, helping themselves to food.

"That's the *voileipäpöytä*," Garth's voice came in her ear. "The cold table, if you prefer a translation. You can have as little or as much as you want."

"Yes, I see." To the side of the large circular table was another, and from the dishes on that, steam rose gently as other kinds of food simmered. And quite suddenly Eve began to feel hungry. The waitress who smilingly handed them their plates was dressed in traditional Lappi costume, predominantly red with colourful embroidery against a background of deep blue, with yellow and white flower patterns embroidered on the red material. Soft-slippered feet, with the theme of flowers again, white-aproned, she was an an impressive picture with just the faintest trace of likeness to Heli in her blonde hair and broad cheekbones.

I've really arrived, Eve thought. I'm *here*, thanks to the man I hired. And the thought was a satisfying one.

The choice was stupefying. Pickled salt herrings, sprats in aspic, fresh salted salmon, cold smoked reindeer, onion rings, a cheese loaf, beetroots, cucumbers, gherkins, tomatoes ... Eve began to feel dizzy with the effort to choose – and then, leaving Garth to work his way around alone, she moved to the hot plates

37

next to her. There were hot oval-shaped pasties lined with mashed potatoes, some with rice, hot pancakes, a succulent-looking stew . . .

Bemused, she helped herself to a pasty, some of the stew, and went back to the cold table to add some salad.

"That's reindeer stew," Garth said cheerfully, but not until she had eaten some. "Like it?"

"It's unusual – no more so than venison," she answered.

"Hmm. Of course. This place isn't licensed, I'm afraid. There's milk or *piimä* – that's sour milk, but very nice with this sort of food – or non-alcoholic beer which I consider pretty ghastly, or I dare say I could persuade a coffee out of them if you really wanted."

"Milk will do fine." She smiled. "I'd hate to be awkward." And for a moment – just a moment, their eyes met. And Eve saw something very puzzling, for a brief second. Had he expected her to want coffee? To *be* awkward?

The moment was gone. It might never have been. But there was no getting away from it. He did puzzle her. And something else happened at the end of the meal, and Eve experienced a twinge, however slight, as if things were being taken out of her hands.

She was about to reach in her handbag for the money to pay when he held up his hand. "Just a second, Eve. I'll pay the bill – and any further ones we encounter."

"You?" She couldn't help the slight raising of her eyebrows. "But you –"

"Yes, I know. I'm working for you. Fine. I'll put all

this on the bill when your trip's over. But I have a rooted, not to say old-fashioned objection to having a woman pay when *I'm* with her." It was there in his voice, a hard male arrogance she didn't like.

Amused, not annoyed, she smiled coolly at him. "What a shame," she said. "To be so terribly old-fashioned, I mean. This *is* the twentieth century, you know, and I have the money to pay my way –"

"Yes, I do know. I've also been employed to look after you, to smooth the way for a rich young lady. The least I can do in my capacity as humble employee is to do just that. And soiling your delicate hands with money is hardly the thing –"

"Don't be so flippant!" she snapped.

"Was I being? And you wouldn't be used to that, would you?" He stood up and pushed his chair under the table. "Come on, let's go. We can continue this argument outside, in the fresh air. The Finns are a very self-contained race, and generally incurious about other people's fights, but I don't see why you should spoil their lunches." And he eased her chair back for her as she rose, then put it neatly under the table.

Incensed, Eve walked quickly out. She turned round, eyes sparkling with anger as he strolled from the restaurant towards her. "How dare you speak to me like that?" she demanded. "How *dare* you!"

He looked her slowly up and down. Very slowly, eyes insolent and mocking. "Quite simple," he answered. "I just don't scare easily, that's all, and *you* – with your arrogant little ways – don't frighten me a bit. And you're stuck with me, and I'm stuck with *you*, and the sooner you accept that fact the easier everything will be –"

"Stuck? With you? Don't be such a fool! If I want, I can sack you *right* now!" she fired at him, eyes hard and cold. "I'll pay you for bringing me here, and say goodbye." And she turned and began to walk towards where they had left the plane.

The next second he caught her arm, forcing her to stop. "No, you can't," he said, and the mockery in his dark grey eyes had turned to that cool amusement she hated about him. "You promised your father that you would use the pilot Esko recommended, and let him take you to your friend – and back to Helsinki. That's *me*."

"How do you know that?" she frowned. "And take your hand off my arm at *once*!" He did so, then laughed.

"Esko told me, that's how. How else?" and he shrugged. Without answering, Eve turned away from him and began to walk on. She couldn't explain the uneasy feeling that filled her. It was the merest whisper of an instinct touching her mind, as of foreboding; a sense of unquiet. But it was as if he had an answer to everything. And it was true. She had promised, and for a moment had been tempted to break that promise – or at least to try to. For with a horrible, helpless sensation, Eve had the feeling that people like Garth Seton didn't get sacked easily. She also realized that she was beginning to dislike him even more intensely than she had imagined she would.

"So why don't we leave the plane where it is for now and go and find your friend's address?" he said.

She slowed her footsteps. In her anger she had almost forgotten the main purpose of her journey. She took a deep breath. "Very well," she answered. "But do you think you could try and be pleasant for a while? It would be such a nice change."

He grinned quickly. "Tell you what, we'll make a pact. A peace pact for the time being, and see how it goes. *You* make the effort to be pleasant – you may find it rewarding, who knows? – and I'll do the same. We may find we actually get on quite well." And he tilted his cap back to an even more rakish angle, and smiled gently, patronisingly, down at her.

"Who knows?" she agreed silkily, resisting the near overwhelming temptation to swipe the smile from his face.

"See? It gets easier as you go along. Right then, shall we find a taxi, or walk?"

They were within sight of the lake, trees and greenery surrounding the water. the pavement was wide and clean-looking, and along the road in front of them, cars and lorries passed, not too frequently, but often enough. The sun was hot, the sky nicely blue and speckled with small, fluffy clouds, and shops and houses the other side of the road were colourful and sharply etched in the clear clean air.

"Let's walk," said Eve. "There's no hurry."

"Fair enough. But if you give me your friend's address I can be asking questions before we start going in the wrong direction."

41

Eve opened her handbag and handed him the sheet of paper on which she had written Heli's name and address, and he looked at it and nodded.

"Okay. Let's go," he said. "We'll cross over here –" and he took her elbow quite casually as they reached the pavement's edge. It was an instinctive gesture, as if to assist her, to prevent her stepping out in front of a white Volkswagen which was being driven swiftly along, and Eve, instead of pulling away, allowed herself to relax. She didn't know how long the "pact" would last, but she wasn't going to spoil it in the first five minutes.

"Have you an idea where it is?" she said, puzzled, as he steered her skilfully through traffic and to the other side.

"I have. It's about five minutes' walk away. I know the street." He had taken his hand away from her arm now, but the memory of his touch was still there, like a small ache. It seemed incredible to Eve. So casual, his tone, as if she had merely taken a short ride to be here, and he was telling her that he knew where Heli lived. Just like that. Like him or not, he was no fool. He knew his way around.

Everywhere was modern, the buildings new and clean, and the people that they passed or overtook in their walking were the same as could be seen in any town in Europe – except for the differences in clothing on some, those who wore Lappi dress, as had the waitress in the restaurant. Not many, but just enough to add colour to the otherwise normally drab neutral street clothes of the other pedestrians. Eve smiled a little as they passed some camera-clicking tourists – clearly American – who appeared to be delighted at a round-faced dark brown-eyed little girl in Lappi costume who stood waiting for her mother outside a shop.

"It's all so modern," Eve remarked to Garth in mild surprise. "I didn't expect a town like this."

"No one does. But Rovaniemi was practically razed to the ground in 1944 – so they rebuilt it. There are very few old buildings, and they stand out. There's a museum in one, full of Stone Age finds, but generally speaking, everything is pretty new." He pointed. "See the railway station in the distance? That's as far north as you can come by train. After here it's bus or flying."

Eve shivered. It was as if she was realizing by that remark just how far north they were. And that reminded her. "How far away is the Arctic Circle?" she asked him. He looked down at her as if wondering why she could possibly be interested in that. But his tone was agreeable enough as he answered.

"Five miles north of here. On the road to Ivalo there's a hut to mark the line. You can buy souvenirs in the kiosk – and postcards which they'll stamp with an Arctic Circle postmark. Perhaps your friend will take you."

"Heli? Perhaps. If she's here," and Eve gave a little smile. Somehow, now she was so very near, the doubts began. And stronger now. It might be a wasted journey – all this way for nothing. Except a few days' respite from – from what? Life? Her life in London? And she said, quickly, because she didn't want to analyse her

43

feelings just *now*: "We'll have to find accommodation soon anyway. I wouldn't expect her to put me up at such short notice."

"Of course not. Nor me," and he grinned crookedly. "But I know one or two places to stay. The hotels up here are good. No problems there."

"I want to stay at the best," she said. She hadn't meant it to come out quite as it did, didn't even realize it until she heard his sharp intake of breath, saw his unconcealed amusement.

"But of course! What else? Do you think I would take you to the sort of place that roughneck adventurers stay? Where boiled potatoes are the staple diet? Perish the thought! Of course you shall stay at the best hotel. It's not far from here, and as you're such an innocent abroad, if you'll pardon the expression, I'll even consider staying there myself, with you – well, no, not exactly with you – please don't get the wrong idea –"

Cutting in, suppressing a rising irritation at the gentle mockery in his voice, Eve said: "You! I certainly don't expect –"

"Ah, before you say it – I'm well aware it's not part of the contract, but I had a good week last week, and a bit of luxury living wouldn't come amiss –"

"Really?" Eve smiled slowly. "I imagined you'd be happier sleeping in one of your wilderness huts –"

"*Autiotupa*? Well done! You remembered. Sorry to disappoint you. It's variety that I like. The spice of life, you know. And occasionally – just occasionally, mind, we peasants like to see how the other half live. It's such a relief to get back to normal again afterwards."

44

"I thought we'd declared a truce? You seem to be doing your best –"

"Okay," he put up his hands in a gesture of surrender. "Point taken. I must not make cracks about the peasantry and the other half any more. Anyway, we're nearly there now. See that street ahead of us?" and he took her arm lightly as he pointed. There was a church on the corner, and everything was well spread out, houses not cramped uncomfortably close, but with space for lawns and trees and flowers. The church was white, dazzling in the sun. Eve blinked.

"I always imagined it would be freezing up here," she said, as they began walking towards their destination. "Instead of which, I'm wishing I'd brought my sunglasses!"

"And you've come at the right time of the year, September. The mosquitoes are vicious up here all summer. They're dying out now."

"Are they?" Eve rubbed her wrist. "Someone should have told the one that just bit me."

"Haven't you brought mosquito cream?" He looked down, frowning.

"No. Nobody told me."

"Hmm. I always carry it in the plane. Remind me after. You'll get used to them after a while. I did."

It was the perfect cue for asking how long he had been working in Finland, but Eve didn't take it. She didn't want to know, she really didn't. After all, she didn't like him, not one little bit, and it was the greatest effort to even be civil to him, let alone start asking personal questions.

"Thanks," she answered.

"Look," he said, as if he had just thought of it, "do you want to go to your friend's on your own? I can hang around, meet you somewhere later –"

"No. I'll need you to translate if – if she's not there –" Eve bit her lip, suddenly feeling vulnerable for the first time in ages.

She felt rather than saw his sudden grin, for the trace of laughter was in his voice when he replied: "As you wish. If, however, she *is* there, I'll make myself scarce. I have one or two pals here I can visit – and I could take her phone number and call you later."

"Yes, that's a good idea." She was amazed at the sense of relief that washed over her at his words. She had never felt this strange sensation – almost like that of being caught on the wrong foot, slightly off balance – before. There was no time to puzzle it out, for they were nearly there now. The street sign, attached to a tree at the corner was unmistakable. "*Lunnankatu*" it said, and Heli lived at number twenty-four, and the houses were all splendid, in their own grounds with well set out gardens. Tall trees shaded them as they walked along a wide pavement, and a youth passed them on a bicycle, whistling some pop tune that had been popular a year or so ago. He too wore a cap similar to Garth's, perched on the back of his head, the only difference being that the top of his was white, not blue. Eve couldn't help the glance from one to the other, could not resist a smile.

"Students' caps," he said. "You'd have seen a lot in

Helsinki if you'd had time to look around, *and* they're mostly like his."

"But you had to be different," she murmured.

"S'right." And he grinned disarmingly at Eve, in that way he had – the way that prickled her skin in an instinctive reaction – but there was nothing you could do about it, for how can you tell someone not to grin?

And then it didn't matter anyway, because they were there. For a moment they stood at the gates and looked up the straight red asphalt driveway to the house, tall, grey, elegant, red-roofed. Eve's heart beat faster. Heli would be here, she *must* be. And then she would see things in perspective again, would know the simple pleasure of talking, of laughter with someone with whom she could relax and be herself. And Garth pushed the white wooden gate open and held it for her. "Right, madame?" he said, half mocking, half serious. Eve walked slowly through and he closed the gate with a decisive "click" behind them.

There was a dusty white Volkswagen parked at an odd angle outside the front entrance. Heli's! Eve laughed. "She's here," she said. "That's her car. She told me in a letter."

"Good," he answered quietly. "Then you won't need me –"

"No. Wait. Just for a minute – please." She didn't know why she should say that, and wondered fleetingly if it was because she wanted to introduce them before he went. So that when she told Heli about this arrogant man, she'd have actually *seen* him for herself . . .

"Okay," he shrugged easily. "As you wish." And he

47

rang the bell beside the red-painted door as Eve followed him more slowly up the stone steps. Silence followed, then a wild barking of dogs, in the distance, coming nearer. The barking stopped abruptly, and Eve knew the dogs were behind the door for there were faint snuffling noises, worse, a spine-chilling rumbling from a dog's throat. And Garth turned to her, his eyes gleaming darkly. "I'll let you go in first," he whispered. "They might not bite women!"

Eve took a deep breath. "Don't be facetious," she hissed.

He raised one eyebrow in mockery. "I'm not," he answered. "I just didn't realize this would be such a dangerous assignment, that's all –"

"Wait. Someone's coming." Eve looked at him, and saw, by his expression, that he had heard it too. Soft, slippered feet approaching slowly, a whispering, then bolts being drawn, with difficulty, one, two, a click, and then, at last, the door swung open a mere three inches and was caught by a chain. And a little elderly face peeped shyly round and in a small voice, said something incomprehensible. Helplessly Eve turned to Garth. She knew she should never have come. It had all gone crazy – surely this couldn't be the right house? Yet there was Heli's car – and the address was hers – so what on earth was going on?

CHAPTER FOUR

An hour later, when they were sitting comfortably in a very elegantly furnished room in Heli's house, Eve felt slightly better. Not much, but at least not as perturbed as when they had waited, unknown and unknowing, outside the house.

She looked across the room to where Garth sat talking to the old woman, and she smiled slowly to herself. To think that she had actually, for a moment or two, been frightened, had felt a trickle of fear run down her back at the two dogs which now lay sprawled asleep on the floor by the window, catching the sun's rays on their backs.

There were just the three of them in the house. No Heli. As she sat listening, but not comprehending their conversation in Finnish, Garth speaking slowly and carefully because the old woman was deaf, Eve's mind went back to the moment when Garth had answered the woman's query, and then turned to Eve as the door had been shut to allow the chain to be taken off. "She asked who we were, so I told her you were Heli's friend from England, Eve Carrick. She knows you."

The hall was surprisingly light and wide, and as she stepped in, the old woman had taken Eve's hand, her face beaming, rosy cheeks shining as she said: "Täti Sofia."

"Aunt Sofia," whispered Garth in translation, and

Eve, smiling, had stooped and impulsively kissed that rosy cheek. "Of course, Heli often mentioned her in letters. Please tell her I'm very pleased to meet her."

And after that it had been all right. The two dogs, giant elkhounds looking like a cross between huskies and wolves, were quite obedient to Aunt Sofia's commands, and seeing that Eve and Garth were not robbers, had led the way into the room where they now sat.

Indirect conversation was quite frustrating, but there was not much choice, for Heli's aunt spoke very little English, and Garth's Finnish was fluent, of that there was no doubt. And gradually the facts had emerged, of which the most important was that Heli was in Geneva with her father, now working for the United Nations, and had been there for two months, and would not be returning for at least two more, when she would spend the winter months with her aunt in Rovaniemi. There was a sick sensation within Eve as all this was told to her by Garth. The waste of time! She could have flown to Geneva had she known, she could have . . . But what was the use of vain regret? She was here now.

Aunt Sofia looked across at Eve as Garth began to repeat her words in English, and she nodded and smiled gently as he spoke, as if she knew exactly what he was saying at any one moment, and was agreeing to it all.

"Aunt Sofia–" it appeared that no one ever called her anything else – "has invited us both to stay for as long as we wish –"

"But –" began Eve.

"And," he continued, ignoring and overriding her interruption, "she will show us round Rovaniemi in Heli's Volkswagen, as Heli left it for her to go shopping in, and she will be only too pleased to do so as Heli often mentioned you and she feels as if she knows you well." No mockery in his voice, none of his usual flippancy in repeating the other's words.

"It's very kind, please tell her, but we can't possibly impose on her in this way." Eve smiled reassuringly at Aunt Sofia as she said it.

She heard Garth's voice, translating, like the voice of a stranger as he spoke this unusual language that came so effortlessly to him, so how had he learned it? And when? And why?

"She would enjoy the company. She's quite alone, except for a daily woman, and the two dogs, and it would be no trouble," and he watched Eve now as he said it, coolly, levelly, because as sure as sure, he knew what was going on in Eve's mind, that she wanted to be away . . .

"All right," she said quickly, before she gave herself time to think. "Tell her thank you very much." And she nodded, and smiled at the little apple-cheeked old lady and wondered what madness had made her accept. Because there was a challenge in Garth's eyes? Because he knew – or thought he knew – that she would refuse? There was no question of him leaving now, and returning later. In a way, he had taken over. Both Aunt Sofia and Eve were dependent on him for their mutual conversation – a fact of which he was well aware. Dark, subtly commanding, yet his manner with the

51

elderly woman was gentle, and Eve found herself drawn irresistibly to watch him. He was no roughneck adventurer, of that she was sure; he had a certainty, an assuredness, about him all the time.

There was no mask that might slip – he was a supremely confident being – and Eve found her dislike of him changing, subtly and unwillingly, to a kind of respect. She had met so very few people in her life who were completely unimpressed by her wealth. Heli had been one. And this man was another. And in an odd way, it was annoying. Which, Eve knew, was completely illogical of her.

"Aunt Sofia wants to know if we're hungry. She's quite concerned because she keeps only enough in the house for her own tastes, which are simple – so I suggested that we all eat out. How does that grab you?"

Eve winced at the blunt expression, then frowned. It was not for *him* to suggest . . . "Well? Don't you like the idea? Speak up."

She couldn't glare at him, as she would have done had they been alone. She contented herself with a silky smile. "You don't give anyone a chance to speak, do you?" she said pleasantly, so that Aunt Sofia would think she was agreeing wholeheartedly. "I was just about to say, *if* you'd given me the chance, that of course it's a good idea. And would you mind not addressing me as if I were a backward child?" she finished, giving the old lady a lovely smile, and inwardly seething at his arrogance. Just when she was deciding that he might not be so revolting after all, he went and put his size ten feet – she looked down at them – no, maybe size eleven – right into it. She had wondered what he would do, going into that beautifully carpeted house wearing clumsy wellingtons. She should, she reflected now as she regarded his grey-socked feet, have known. He had, with a few brief words to Aunt Sofia, taken them off and left them neatly in the hall and then padded on into the lounge for all the world as if that was the *only* way to behave.

He was translating again, had turned away to do so even as she finished speaking to him, so that she wasn't sure if he heard the reprimand – and it was certain that he wouldn't care if he had. Eve sighed a little sigh. Nobody had made her come. It was all her own idea. But oh, how she wished she had telephoned from London, instead of coming on blind impulse, as she had. And who would have answered the phone? Aunt Sofia, deaf and not speaking English? There would have been a way to find out, there always was. A call to Esko and Liisa, and they would soon have sorted the situation out, and Eve could have gone straight to Geneva, and then she wouldn't have had to put up with this Garth Seton, this amused, watchful stranger who was filling her with very mixed feelings indeed. She knew what one of the sensations was anyway. It was that of being left out of things, of being a mere spectator. Eve didn't like that, because she wasn't used to it. Wherever she went, she was the centre of attention, and she was accustomed to it and expected it. Now, sitting and watching the dark Garth talking, she thought fleetingly: they wouldn't even miss me if I went out. The old lady chuckled and nodded, highly amused, and Eve felt a stab of annoyance touch her. Who the hell did he think he was?

"Okay, we'll go in about an hour. Meantime she'll show us our rooms. I've explained where your luggage is, and we'll collect it when we go out to eat." Garth stood up and looked down at Eve.

"Oh, will we?" She had had enough. "And suppose I want to change *before* we go out to eat?"

He cocked her a crooked grin. "Suppose you do? Then I reckon I can go to the plane now in the Volkswagen and collect it – *boss*."

"I asked you not to call me that," she said, temper rising fast.

He nodded. "So you did, so you did. But I reckon that's what I'll call you when you start cracking the whip. There are pleasanter ways of telling me that you'd like your luggage – why don't you try one some time?" And he turned away from her and spoke to the old woman. His back was to Eve, he bent solicitously to talk to Aunt Sofia, and it was expressive. I don't give a solitary damn about you, it said with an eloquence that was as clear as his words might have been.

Then he turned slowly again to face her. "I'm going now," he said, dark eyes on Eve, unblinking, cool. "You'll just have to mime while I'm gone, won't you?" And he followed the old woman from the room and closed the door after him. He didn't say how long he would be. Eve lifted her chin. I'm paying him, she thought. He's working for *me*. There's no reason why he shouldn't go and fetch *my* cases. But she wished that she hadn't spoken.

54

Eve spoke to Heli on the telephone that evening after they had returned from their meal in Rovaniemi. Aunt Sofia had told them that Heli or her father rang every night at ten when they were away, just to check that everything was all right, so they had timed the dinner to enable them to return in good time.

Garth drove the Volkswagen, Aunt Sofia being quite happy to let him do so, and he had taken them to a hotel on the outskirts of the town where they had eaten another enormous meal – and Aunt Sofia had surprised them both by her capacity for both food and drink. The hotel was licensed, and Eve drank wine with her meal, and vodka afterwards with her coffee. Garth did not drink at all, and she had been unable to hide her surprise at that.

"If you drink and drive in this country you go to prison," he had explained patiently, raising his coffee cup in a mocking salute as she sipped her vodka. "I don't want to go to prison, so –" and he shrugged, "when I'm driving or flying I stay teetotal."

"But just a little?" she asked. "Can't you have just one drink?"

"No, not one. There's no legal minimum of alcohol. Drivers can be stopped any time, anywhere – and if you've taken alcohol you've *had it*. And it's not just prison, it's work. They put you to work on roads or airports for a few weeks. It happened to a friend of mine," he added reflectively, "and he'd only had two beers. Mind you, he was fitter when he came out than when he'd gone in, but I'll do my exercise the easy way, isometrics, not digging up roads."

Eve believed him. There was a ruthless simplicity in the law. She shook her head. Suppose, just suppose, no one had told her, and she had hired a car, and driven after just *one* vodka ... the thought of prison was sobering. Money bought most things, and fines were easy to pay, but to have no choice ...

And he must have read her mind again. "Don't worry," he said, as he watched her put her glass down. "You're not driving. I am."

And that had effectively closed the subject. Aunt Sofia was happily tired and content as they drove home. It was nearly ten, and the lights they had left on shone in greeting as Garth took the car up the drive. The air had a fresh cold clarity to it, and Eve breathed deeply as she stood waiting for Garth to help Aunt Sofia out. She looked up at the star-filled sky and an ache of longing for something – she knew not what – filled her. It was like loneliness – yet she was rarely alone. It was a sense of desolation – yet why should it be? She was wealthy and beautiful and popular. And yet, just for a second, it had been there, and it was disturbing.

Then the door was open, the dogs were greeting them, being allowed out for their last run of the day, and warmth and golden light spilled out from the hall, dispelling Eve's brief sadness, chasing it away into the surrounding darkness and shadows. She followed Aunt Sofia in, and then turned to watch Garth close the door. He had brought his own case from the plane with hers. He wore shoes instead of the wellingtons, and had changed from jeans into trousers and a sports jacket over a blue roll-necked sweater. Casual wear, but she had seen women look at him in the hotel with more than a flicker of interest in their eyes. The scar added to rather than detracted from any attraction he might possess, Eve had to admit that.

"The call should come soon, Eve, Aunt Sofia says. She's going to make coffee while we're waiting, and I'm going to help her, so you might as well sit down." And with that he followed Heli's aunt towards the kitchen, leaving Eve feeling faintly – and ever so subtly – unwanted again. She would have enjoyed helping, seeing the kitchen, but she wasn't going to volunteer. He'd made it clear enough: you're not needed.

Speaking to Heli was so good that nothing else mattered. Her voice came across the many miles as clearly as if she were in the next room.

"Oh, Eve, it is good to speak to you. Such a surprise! Why did you not write?"

"I did, several weeks ago. Your aunt told us she forwarded the letter to your address in Geneva –"

"Ah, but it did not arrive! What a shame you have travelled so far on a wasted journey like that. If only I had known!"

"It's my own fault, Heli. But I just wanted to get away for a while –" she was going to add: "You know how it is," but stopped herself. Heli would not know how it was – and that was part of her charm, her calm bright acceptance of life, her placid nature, so soothing to one whose nerves were jangled from the turmoil of London life. Instead Eve said: "Your aunt has made us very welcome. I'll stay for a couple of days and then go home." She knew that Garth would be listening. The telephone was in the wide hall, quite near to the lounge where he was sitting drinking coffee with Aunt Sofia, and they were not talking. The old woman was awaiting her turn on the telephone to speak to her niece.

"Yes. Aunt Sofia has given you my room, I suppose? Good. Then look in the second long drawer of the dressing table. You will find something to amuse you. Oh, it is so good to talk again! I thought that we had lost touch, and that is not good. I would have written anyway at Christmas, but I imagined you would be too busy to write . . ." They spoke for a short while after, knowing there would be the call the following evening, and then Eve passed the telephone to Aunt Sofia and went to have her coffee. "Too busy to write" – no condemnation there on Heli's part, just a simple comment.

She was engrossed in her thoughts and Garth's voice was an intrusion. He had shut the door to the hall after the old woman, and they could hear her voice faintly, speaking quickly, obviously pleased, for she occasionally laughed, and Eve wondered what she was telling Heli . . .

"So we're staying a couple of days, are we?"

She looked up from her coffee cup. "Yes. Why?"

He shrugged. "Idle curiosity. We'll be leaving Monday, will we?"

"Probably. Is that convenient for you?"

"Oh, sure." He smiled. "I'll phone Esko and Liisa to tell them on Monday morning, shall I? You'll stay there

58

in Helsinki a night before flying back to London, I take it? And then will you go and visit Heli in Geneva?"

"Possibly." Eve felt vague irritation rising in her at his questions. "But I don't see what business it is of yours –"

"None at all, actually. I'm just nosey, or hadn't I told you that?" He was laughing. Not openly, not that rudely, but near enough to it.

And suddenly Eve had had enough. She was tired, not only with travelling, and she didn't feel like sparring with this man. Her cases were in her bedroom, all she had to do was go. She stood up. "I hope you'll excuse me," she said. "I'm going to bed. Will you say good night to Aunt Sofia for me?" and before he could answer she turned and went out and ran upstairs as if pursued. Aunt Sofia, busy talking, didn't even notice.

Eve closed the bedroom door and crossing to the dressing table, opened the drawer that Heli had told her. Neatly folded underclothes filled the space – almost. There was just room for a large book, which Eve lifted out carefully. It was a photograph album. She opened it and knew why Heli had told her about it. Inside were dozens of photographs of their old school, taken over a period of two or three years. Eve began to smile as she recognised familiar faces. Heli had always had a camera, had spent hours busily snapping away – and here were the results. She put her hand to her mouth to stifle a giggle as she saw the group of five dressed in eighteenth-century costume for a period play. Who on earth was that one at the back? Eve bit her lip. Fiona? No – Charlotte. Of course! Charlotte, the dizzy blonde who at eighteen had married a millionaire and was now living on a ranch in Texas. Mummy and Daddy, titled, had not been very pleased ... The memories came flooding back, some warm and nostalgic, some sad, because that brief happy time was gone for ever and nothing would bring it back. Nothing.

And when the tap came at the door, she answered: "Come in," without thinking that Aunt Sofia wouldn't understand. But it wasn't her, it was Garth, and he entered and said: "I thought you were tired."

"What do you want?" She put the book down on the bed.

"Toothpaste. I've lost mine. Please." Then she saw that he carried a toothbrush, and had a towel slung over his shoulder. She looked at him, still a little lost in the world contained in the photographs. What would Heli make of him? One thing was certain – her aunt liked him. Maybe Heli, with her pleasant ways, would do so as well. But then maybe he wouldn't be rude to *her*.

"No? You only have to refuse, you know. I shan't go storming out in temper –"

"I was thinking. There's a tube on the dressing table. Take it. If you leave it in the bathroom I'll collect it when I go." And then she looked at her watch, surprised that he should have come up to bed so soon after her – and saw that over an hour had passed. She had been sitting looking at the photographs all that time, and it had seemed like a few minutes ...

"And our rooms are next door to one another. So if

you need anything during the night, you only have to call." She looked up swiftly, but the blandness of his expression gave nothing away.

"I won't," she stood up, "but it's very kind of you to offer. I shall feel somehow – safer – knowing you're so close." She didn't try to disguise the sarcasm, and added softly: "And thanks for telling me. I'll make sure I *lock* my door."

He picked up the tube of toothpaste from the dressing table, half turned, looked at Eve very levelly and coolly from beneath those dark brows. "I assure you you're in no danger from me." And his eyes slowly took in the length of her in hard assessment. It was the look in them that was so expressive. The look that said as clearly – perhaps even more explicitly – than words: "I don't fancy *you* at all."

No man had ever looked at her like that before. Men's eyes lingered on her face and form, and she could almost read their minds, and some had been more outspoken and told her what they thought of her, and she was used to that. But no man had ever dismissed her in one brief precise glance before. She stepped forward, cheeks pink. "Get out," she said.

"Just like that?" he began to grin. "Why? Because I made it clear that I'm not lusting after you? What am I to make of you? Am I to take it you'd have been less annoyed if I'd made a pass –"

He caught her upraised arm before it got anywhere near his cheek. "Ah – ah, *temper*! Nice girls don't go around smacking men's faces. Not without good reason anyway. And I hardly think that assuring you of my honourable intentions constitutes a good reason –"

"Let *go* of my arm!" Incensed, Eve tugged herself free. "And get out *at once*. How dare you speak to me like that! You are grossly impertinent –"

"I already told you, I dare easily – with you. But I'm going anyway. I can't stand here all night talking – and I can see that I've interrupted your session of nostalgia with your old school photos." He reached up his hand and tapped her chin gently. "Back you go to the memories – who knows, it might make you sweeter-tempered to remember what you were like in those young innocent days –"

"How did you know?" She was still breathing hard.

"Aunt Sofia told me Heli mentioned she'd like to see your face when you opened the book. And anyway, I can hardly miss those, can I?" And he nodded gently towards the still open book on the bed. "There's something unmistakably *English* about those type of schoolgirl photos."

She couldn't help herself. She looked down at the pages full of photos. He'd spoilt it now. "Please go," she said more quietly. She felt exhausted, as if she had run a long distance.

"Of course I will. Good night, dear Eve. Pleasant dreams." And she heard the door close behind him, but she didn't look up. How she loathed him!

Whenever Eve had the fleeting thought, the next day, that she could have been on her way back to Helsinki instead of wasting time, she would look at Aunt Sofia's face – and the selfish thought would go. For the old lady was clearly enjoying herself immensely, rosy cheeks glowing as she told Garth – who then translated it to Eve – where exactly they were. And it was Aunt Sofia who had helped to bring Heli up after Heli's own mother died, Aunt Sofia who had, in a way, helped Heli become the person she now was. It was a small enough return for Eve to make, to share a couple of her days with this old lady.

The only snag was Garth, of course, but even he was making an effort, as if he knew, and much to Eve's surprise, she found that she was enjoying her day immensely, when, in the middle of the afternoon, they stopped for coffee and biscuits at a *baari*, after visiting the Arctic hut. Eve had written a postcard to her father there, although she thought there was the possibility she would arrive home before it. Then she had wandered round the racks of picture postcards debating whether to send anyone else one.

John? Neil? They thought she was mad to go dashing off anyway. John in particular couldn't imagine anything drearier than the Arctic Circle. "For heaven's sake, darling," he had said, when Eve had told him. "What's there? Trees and lakes – yuk!" But John would never understand the urge to get away anyway, because he never did. London, and the occasional trip to the Riviera, were all he ever asked from life; his whole world revolved round racehorses, gambling, nightclubbing and keeping in well with his father, because one day he would inherit a small fortune. And Neil. Eve's fingers hovered over a card depicting the Aurora Borealis in glorious Technicolor. At least Neil had a sense of humour, something she now realized with almost a sense of shock that John lacked.

"Let me go with you," he had begged when she told him, and she had been almost tempted, except that her father and Neil didn't see eye to eye, and she had told Daddy she was going by herself. "No," she had answered. "Daddy thinks I'm going alone." And Neil, without batting an eyelid, had come back with: "If we get married first, he'll not mind." He was always proposing. As was John, for that matter, and they detested each other heartily. And Eve, sitting in the *baari* afterwards, drinking hot delicious coffee, had thought back then to John and Neil and wondered what they were doing. And suddenly, to her great surprise, she found that she didn't care, couldn't even summon up the memory of their faces, only as two vague blurs. But another face was sharply defined in her mind's eye, so clearly that she did not have to turn and look at the man buying more coffees at the counter for them. Now why, she thought, should Garth Seton's face be so vividly in my mind when I can't stand him? And as he returned, carefully balancing three beakers of coffee, she looked up at him. That *stupid* cap was annoying her more each day. She was beginning to feel sure he knew, and wore it all the more rakishly simply to annoy her.

"There you are, ladies," he said, and pulled up his stool beside Aunt Sofia who sat there in an old but very warm-looking fur coat – for the day was surprisingly cool – and sat down. Then he looked across the table at Eve, and grinned. "Where to now?" he asked.

Eve shrugged. "Ask Aunt Sofia," she said. "I don't mind at all." And she didn't. She was, despite *him*, enjoying herself. More, she felt as if certain tensions of the past few weeks were draining away from her, reducing in importance as they faded slowly. She pondered on that. Why should it be? she wondered, as she half listened to the two busily discussing where they should go next. This man is more of an irritant than anything, and yet – and yet – I feel quite relaxed, as I haven't done for ages, with the two of them.

And at that moment he looked up, straight into her eyes, and it was as if he knew. Sooty-lashed eyes, dark, the greyness with a smoky quality, narrowed slightly as he looked at Eve, and her heart gave a little quickened beat because she saw for the very first time a smouldering sensuality in them, a dark awareness of his own virility. He's all man, she thought – I never saw it before, but now I know. Which made it all the more strange that he should never have looked upon her with the warmth, the desire she expected to see in a man's eyes. Then the expression was gone, shuttered, the eyes cool and watchful – and nothing else.

"Are you all right?" he said.

"I'm fine," answered Eve, though not with absolute truth, for she was vaguely disturbed. "Have you decided?"

"Yes. A visit to a lake, then shopping. Aunt Sofia would like to make us a traditional Finnish dinner tonight."

65

"Fine." Eve nodded her agreement, and smiled at the old woman. On a sudden impulse that she didn't understand herself, she reached out and laid her hand on the other's. "Please tell her how grateful I am for all her kindness," she said to Garth, without looking at him.

He spoke the words meaningless to Eve, but she saw Aunt Sofia's face soften, saw the beginnings of the smile, watched it grow, as she nodded and answered him swiftly.

"She says," he translated, voice cool and expressionless, "that she is only too happy to have you here, such a dear friend of Heli's, and that her house is yours for as long as you wish to stay."

Eve swallowed. "Thank you," she whispered. There was an inexplicable lump in her throat, an aching sadness for she knew not what, a strange sensation for her.

"Tell her yourself," suggested Garth. "The Finnish is *Kiitos.*"

"*Kiitos*, Aunt Sofia," said Eve, and the old lady chuckled delightedly and caught Eve's hand.

"*Kyllä,*" she said. "*Kiitos*, Eve." Her face shone with simple pleasure. And Garth stood up. "If you've finished your coffee," he said. "We'd better go." He was looking at his watch, not Eve, for which she was thankful. Because she preferred him not to see the faint blurriness from tears in her eyes. She was in no mood for his mockery, yet she could imagine it. The strange thing was, she couldn't understand why she should have been so moved by a trivial incident. Perhaps I'm getting soft, she thought, as she followed the other two out of the café. I wonder why that should be? And the question was whipped away by a sharp breeze, and then forgotten as she took a deep breath at the coldness of the air, and walked towards the Volkswagen.

CHAPTER FIVE

Eve awoke on Sunday morning with a thumping headache, and at first could not understand why. Then she remembered, and groaned softly, turning on one side in bed to see if the men with little hammers might leave her temples alone. Aunt Sofia had persuaded the daily woman to stay and help her prepare the meal the previous evening. Then she had made several phone calls. Eve winced now in remembrance. What had started out as a quiet evening had developed into a party of heroic proportions – one which, she now realized in retrospect, she had enjoyed immensely. In fact, she thought, as she struggled to sit up, she couldn't remember when she had enjoyed an evening more. If only the little men would go away . . .

"You awake, Eve?" Garth's voice, then his head appeared round the open doorway. Eve lay down again, and he walked in and looked down at her, and shook his head gently.

"Oh dear, oh dear," he said. "You certainly know how to knock back the *Koskenkorva*. And look at you now. Do you want some coffee?"

"What *Kosk* – er – *Kosken* – what are you talking about?" she managed groggily.

"Finnish schnapps. You and that fellow, Jussi – you remember, the handsome one you kept telling everyone reminded you of Burt Reynolds – were knocking it back in the corner like nobody's business."

The mists were clearing rapidly. And Eve smiled, remembering Jussi. What a charmer he had been! For the phone calls had all been to various friends of Heli's, and they had turned up, nine or ten young people in their early twenties, and, an added bonus, all speaking good English. But Jussi, ah, Jussi! A little smile curled Eve's mouth. "Yes," she said, "I remember now. That explains the headache. But never mind," and she looked up at Garth. "It was worth it."

"Was it? At one point I thought he was going to nibble your ear off. Still, there's no accounting for taste, I always say. I'll get your coffee," and with that he turned and went out. Eve frowned. Now what had been in his voice then? Certainly not jealousy – *that* was a funny thought to have. Disapproval? Perhaps, he pulled a little face to herself. Heavens above, if he got into a tizzy about a little harmless flirtation he must be a very old-fashioned fellow. No one else had noticed, or bothered. The record player had been going full blast, everyone dancing – even Aunt Sofia was persuaded to leave her chair by the fire – the dogs hiding in a quiet corner, and the whole atmosphere had been fantastic.

She pondered on that. What a contrast to the parties to which she was accustomed, much more sophisticated affairs with a group, and a buffet table, and her own circle of friends – and this, an impromptu get-together, unplanned, with complete strangers. John and Neil would have been like fish out of water. Garth had not. It was as if he *belonged*. Yet they were as much strangers to him. In a way he had been like a host, helping Aunt Sofia, organising things. . . He's the man I hired to *fly* me up here, thought Eve in sudden irritation. So who the hell does he think he is, taking over, criticizing my behaviour? Just who. . . And he walked in at that moment, the subject of her thoughts, carrying a hot beaker full of coffee, and said:

"Right now, you'd better sit up," and he flung her wrap at her. "Put that on if you're worried about me staring, although I assure you I won't be."

She grabbed the silk dressing gown and pulled it on. "Your manners leave a lot to be desired," she said coolly.

"Yes, I know. Sorry I'm not a smoothie, but you'll have to take me as you find me. Anyway, I'll bet Jussi can't fly a plane –"

"Nobody was talking about Jussi – " she began.

"Ah, *you* weren't, but I was. I could see that *his* manners charmed you no end, in fact you were positively lapping it up, I noticed, and who's to blame you? It's not every day you get handsome Finns trying to eat you –"

"Shut up!" she grated. "Just shut up. *Please.*" Her eyes sparkled angrily. If he didn't –

"Zowie! What a girl! Perhaps he likes spitfires. Who knows? No accounting for –"

"You already said that. Taste. Yes, I know. Have you been reading too many American comics – or is it television?" she asked as sweetly as possible. "You

70

sound like Batman, it's frightfully *boring*," she finished. If that didn't squash him once and for all, nothing would.

And he began to laugh, then sat down on the bed, as if helpless. "Oh, Eve," he managed at last. "If you could see your face! Pity Jussi didn't. He'd know the kitten could spit as well as purr –"

That did it. He was sitting on *her* bed, laughing at *her*. Eve jerked her leg down sharply and felt it make satisfying contact with his side.

"Get *out*. *Now*, " she breathed. "You are quite the rudest –"

But she didn't finish, because his hand had imprisoned her ankle underneath the eiderdown, and he held it, not tightly, but not tenderly either.

"Don't try and kick me, miss," he warned, but still with that infuriating trace of laughter in his voice. "Or I'll pull your leg down so fast you'll wonder what happened."

"You wouldn't –" she began.

"I would. Try me," he offered. "I'd like to see you explain to Aunt Sofia how you managed to spill all your coffee over yourself. And what a waste! *I* made it, and it's good. So drink up like a good girl and I can take your beaker and wash it. You see, Aunt Sofia has gone to church and I don't see why she should have to wash up after us when she returns."

Smouldering, resisting the very strong urge to throw the coffee over him, Eve began to drink it. The man was too impossible for words! She felt and saw his hand leave her ankle and he rubbed his chin thoughtfully.

"Mmm," he said, as if pondering. "One more day here, and then back to Helsinki."

"Thank goodness," she breathed, and he cocked a dark eyebrow at her.

"Meaning you'll be glad to get rid of me? Hmm, I see. Why don't you say so outright, instead of muttering under your breath?"

"I'll be glad to get rid of you," she said in clear tones. "There, does that suit you?"

"It'll do," he replied, not a bit abashed. "Have you finished your coffee?"

"Nearly. You don't have to wait. I'm perfectly capable of washing a beaker –" she stopped as he smote his brow in pretended horror, and sat back.

"*You!* Wash a *beaker!* Heaven forbid that I should allow *that*. Why, I've been hired to look after you, and I intend to do just that –"

"Then why don't you shut up and get on with it?" she interrupted. "Because for a hired hand, I find you remarkably insolent. Not only that, you're sitting on my bed, which I definitely don't like, in my bedroom, which is one place I would have thought I could find a certain degree of privacy – and not only *that*," she went on, her eyes sparkling as she warmed to her theme and completely forgot any lingering traces of headache, "but you seem to feel as if you have the freedom to pop in and out as you please, like some jack-in-the-box, *and* as well, you managed to take complete charge of the party last night, like some hired M.C. or something, and I find you quite the most exasperating man I've ever met *in my life*, and if you don't go *at once*, I shall hit you, because I've just about had enough of you!" and with that she slammed her empty beaker down on the bedside table and glared hard at him.

Garth jumped to his feet. He seemed to be having difficulty in swallowing, and for a moment Eve wondered if he was about to choke. Then she saw that he was trying to suppress laughter. In vain. The next moment it exploded as he flung back his head and roared with it. It was the last straw. The very last straw. Eve jumped out of bed, pulled the silk wrap more tightly round her, marched over to him and began to pummel his chest and arms with her fists. "I hate –" she began, and was stopped before she could finish because suddenly he wasn't helpless with laughter any more; he had grabbed her arms and was holding her and looking now down at her. Then he shook his head gently, chidingly.

"Oh dear, oh dear," he said softly. "You shouldn't have done that, you know. You really shouldn't. Just because I was laughing at your outrageous remarks. It's no way to behave, going round hitting people –"

"Let me go at once!" she said, because he had a grip like steel and he was hurting her arms.

"When you apologise –"

"To you! Go to hell," she stormed – and kicked his leg with her bare foot – and instantly wished she hadn't, for two reasons, one because it hurt her toes – his leg was *hard*, and two, because the next second she found herself floating in a rather graceful way to land on the bed with Garth still imprisoning her but now on top of her.

73

"Judo," he said, and his eyes gleamed darkly. "You must learn never to kick a judo black belt because you'll land flat on your back. And now I have you quite helpless, are you going to apologise?"

"No," she said. "To you, never –" and the end of the word tailed away because his mouth came down on ·hers. And he kissed her. Not in a way she had ever been kissed before, and Eve had been kissed often. This was different, oh, quite different. Because for a start he hadn't shaved, and it was like sandpaper on her skin, and *that* had never happened before, but more, his kiss wasn't tender or gentle, it was hard and ruthless – and exciting.

And when she knew that last fact, Eve began to struggle, resenting her treacherous response. And then he released her and jerked her up into a sitting position.

His teeth gleamed as he grinned at her. "Had enough?" he enquired.

She touched her cheeks and chin. "You brute," she said. "You've rubbed my skin raw."

"Is that all you can say? Serves you right. Don't hit me – or kick me again." He tapped her chin. "And don't tell me I'm fired either, because we've only got another twenty-four hours to put up with each other, and I'm sure you can manage that. And another thing, little hell-cat, try and be nice to Aunt Sofia today. *I* like her."

"So do I!" Eve exclaimed indignantly. She would think about the awful kiss later, when she was alone. She wanted him to go first. "Why do you say that?"

He looked down at her sitting on the bed, thoughtfully. "No reason. I don't want you taking it out on her just because *we* have our differences of opinion –"

"Don't be stupid," she cut in. "Why should I? She's my friend's aunt. She is our hostess – and she even likes you, though I would have thought she'd have better taste –"

"Ah, ah!" He put up a finger in a warning gesture. "Let's not start again. We'll have a truce for today, I think. That should be a pleasant change. So long – boss," and he took the beaker and walked quickly out of the bedroom and closed the door behind him.

Eve lay back and let her mind go back over the events of the last few minutes. Her body still tingled from the contact and she was in a turmoil. It had all happened so swiftly that it was difficult to get everything in any sort of order. There was just this overwhelming sense of breathlessness within her – and a kind of shock. No man had ever dared to treat her like this before. No man had ever retaliated as swiftly or powerfully as he – and she hated him, had done before he'd kissed her – so why was there this treacherous weakness as the image of his dark intent face swam into view? Why the vaguely disturbing sensations within her? Her face still tingled from the roughness of his beard, and yet in an odd way, that was no longer unpleasant. She touched her mouth carefully. His lips had been cool and dry – not so the kiss. She had previously looked at him and thought: he's all man. Now she knew it for a fact.

Suddenly irritated with herself for her thoughts, Eve stood up and went for a towel and soap. When she went downstairs, he would see that she wasn't one jot bothered by anything *he* could do. She paused by the mirror before she went out to the bathroom. Her cheeks were faintly pink, her eyes clear and lustrous. All hangover gone. A reluctant smile curved her mouth as she looked at herself. If he was good for nothing else, at least he was an effective headache curer, she thought. Then she went to have a wash.

She and Heli had spoken only briefly, the previous night, because the party was in full swing at ten o'clock, and the noise was not conducive to good conversation. But now, Sunday evening, after a day spent sightseeing round Rovaniemi, Eve was able to speak properly to her friend.

"How did it go?" was Heli's first question, and Eve laughed.

"Oh, Heli, how I wish you'd been here. You have some super friends. It was marvellous. And Aunt Sofia was dancing all night! When I came here I thought she looked so frail, but she has more stamina than all of us put together."

"I know! And what of your mystery man – Garth – is that his name? She was telling me about him when we spoke on Friday evening, but I could not ask you last night because of the noise. But Aunt Sofia is very taken with him and tells me how very attractive he is. So! Eve! What are the secrets you are keeping from your friend Heli?" but her voice held laughter.

Eve had been going hot and cold while the other spoke, darting glances towards the lounge where Garth and Aunt Sofia were watching a film on television, as if he might almost hear Heli's words. And how could she reply? The sound on the television wasn't very loud.

"Just a second, Heli," she said, and darting across, closed the door. Let him think what he liked! She wasn't going to talk about him while he was actually listening.

"Hello? Oh, I shut the door. Um – well, I hired him to fly me up here, Heli. I promised my father I'd get someone that Esko recommended, and it was him."

"But he is very handsome, is he not? Has he fallen for you, Eve?"

Eve swallowed. "No! Of course not! Heavens," she tried a little laugh but it wasn't very convincing, "he's just a pilot, you know, someone I've hired. He's very helpful as a translator, of course – anyway, I'll tell you all about it when I see you. It's difficult to talk now –" she paused.

"Ah! I understand. He can hear you? Yes, of course, Eve. I'm looking forward to seeing you in Geneva. You have my phone number and address? Good."

"Yes. I'll phone you as soon as I get home to London, and we'll fix something up. Then we'll talk. I've so much to tell you, Heli."

"And I you! The social life here is very good. You will have a wonderful time when you come, Eve, I promise you. . ."

They spoke for several more minutes, and then it was Aunt Sofia's turn and Eve went thoughtfully back into the darkened lounge. Parties in Geneva, Heli had said, but Eve knew that wasn't what she wanted. She

77

was bored with parties. All she craved was peace and quiet, and to talk to Heli. And Heli would understand when Eve told her why. She always did, always had. That was what made her such a special friend; one who listened, and sensed the right thing to say – one who cared.

Eve sighed a little sigh and sat down. The film was an American one, a Cary Grant–Doris Day comedy, and it was funny to hear them speaking such fluent Finnish – and quite incomprehensible to Eve, so she sat back and contented herself with watching. The set was a splendidly large colour set, but superbly designed and simple, not ornate.

"Tired, Eve?"

She opened her eyes quickly. It had only been for a second, and she had been thinking about things. . . "Not at all. Why? Are you?" She had treated him coolly all day, a difficult feat when he was the only interpreter, but she wasn't going to let him think he'd got away with anything. When they parted at Helsinki tomorrow, she would tell him a few things about himself that he didn't know. And with any luck they wouldn't see one another again.

"Me? I'm never tired. What time do you want to leave in the morning?"

"As early as possible," she retorted dryly.

"Hmm, and I won't ask *why*," was his equally dry response. "We'll ask Aunt Sofia when she comes in, shall we?"

"Yes."

And so it was arranged. Aunt Sofia would drive them

to their plane immediately after breakfast. And Eve went to bed that night knowing that she would soon be back home. As she slid into bed the thought came to her: In another day I'll have said farewell to that awful man. And her heart gave a sudden little lurch that made her frown slightly. She lay back on the cool pillows. It would be a relief, wouldn't it, to get away from him? Of *course* it would. People like him were best avoided. He was arrogant, domineering, rude – and not averse to using force on a woman – completely unlikeable – so why, she thought, did that strange feeling go through her at the thought of saying goodbye? But there was no one to answer that. Certainly not Eve.

She woke early the next day because of a slight sound – a door being unlocked. She looked at her watch. It was nearly seven o'clock. On an impulse she went across and drew back one curtain – to see Garth walking down the red drive from the house. Eve blinked and looked at her watch again. No, she hadn't been mistaken, it was five minutes to seven. So where was he going? There was no other sound from the house. Presumably Aunt Sofia still slept. And the dogs. A wave of intense curiosity swept through Eve. Because there had been something very purposeful about his walk; not a gentle stroll, but swift long strides. Sleep was out of the question. She turned and looked at the bed, then let the curtain fall into place. Her packing was done. A leisurely bath seemed a very good idea. And in it, she would be able to think.

Eve had brought a small present for Heli, a box of exquisite hand-made chocolates from a Bond Street shop. She gave them to Aunt Sofia after breakfast, and the old woman's reception of them was touching. She stood on tiptoe to kiss Eve's cheek, and then hugged her. Garth's translation wasn't needed. "Please tell her I'll write as soon as I get home," Eve said to Garth. They were all standing in the large sunny kitchen, having a last cup of coffee before leaving, and the two dogs sprawled on the carpet by the huge open fire, fast asleep.

The cases were in the hall. All that remained was to leave. And, as they went through the front door into cool frosty sunlight, Eve looked back. In a strange way, even without Heli, the weekend had done her good. Yet it was difficult to explain why. They had seen Rovaniemi, been for rides, had a marvellous party – and she and Garth had sustained their brittle relationship with occasional lapses into – into what? Violence? Almost. Her skin could tingle at the sight of him – even, sometimes, at the thought of him. And where *had* he been on his walk? She had heard him come back into the house as she dried herself after her bath. He had been away nearly an hour.

She sat in the rear of the car and watched the back of his head. It really doesn't matter, of course, she thought. In a few hours we'll have kissed each other goodbye, metaphorically speaking – and he can go to the moon for all I care. And she gave a little shiver at that moment because somehow the thought affected her most oddly. Aunt Sofia was driving, and her pace was slow, and Eve had time to look around her at the other houses in the road. A man washing his car waved as they passed, and Aunt Sofia tooted in reply, and the atmosphere was quite a leisurely one. Almost like parts of England, thought Eve, as they neared a crossroads, and the church was beside them – and something else. A telephone box.

And then she knew. She knew where Garth had gone on his walk, knew it as surely as if he had told her. It was the right distance away from the house, and Garth had turned right at the gate, as they had just done, and there were no shops that he could have been to, for a newspaper or cigarettes. Don't be silly, she chided herself. Why should he go out to make a phone call when Aunt Sofia would let him phone from the house? And she looked back, out of the rear window, and Garth said with a brightly innocent tone: "That's a phone box." He turned round to look into her eyes. And then he smiled, as if he knew.

"Thank you for telling me," she answered. "You're a mine of information." He was waiting for her to ask something else – and Eve was determined not to give him the satisfaction. She wanted to make a joke of it – to say it resembled a kind of mini-time machine, as in *Doctor Who*, because the structure was a weird-looking one of aluminium and glass – but she wouldn't. She might have with anyone else – but not him. Because she had a strange feeling about it all – but she didn't know why.

CHAPTER SIX

AND then, at last, they were in the air, and Rovaniemi grew smaller and more distant as they circled the town and set out towards Helsinki. The last farewells had been almost sad. Aunt Sofia had told Eve, through Garth, that she hadn't enjoyed herself so much for ages – and Eve felt sure that she wasn't just saying it out of politeness. There was an open invitation for her any time she chose to come – and then she had added something which was clearly intended for Garth, for he had answered her without bothering to translate to Eve. And this last fact was irritating Eve so much that she eventually said, after several minutes of silence in which only the throbbing engines could be heard: "What did Aunt Sofia say to you?"

"I thought you'd never ask," he commented. "In fact I was getting *worried* –"

"Don't bother –" she began stiffly, regretting the weakness.

"But of course. She was telling me to visit her next time I was in Rovaniemi. She knows I have friends there."

Of course! Perhaps he'd been phoning *them*! Eve hadn't considered that. It was a perfectly logical explanation, especially if he had something private to say. "Lost your tongue?" his words brought her back to the present.

"Not at all. I was thinking, that's all. Tell me, have you prepared a bill for me?"

"Not yet. I can tell you how much you owe when we arrive in Helsinki. Are you intending to visit Esko and Liisa or go straight home?"

And she remembered something else then that he had said. "Ah, was it them you went to telephone this morning?"

"What do you mean?" He looked at her from his position at the controls, this cool, aggressive self-assured man, and even now his question had a hard edge to it.

She shrugged. There wasn't much he could do to her while he had to concentrate on flying. "I saw you set out at seven from the house, and I heard you come back while I was bathing. And when we passed that telephone box, I guessed where you'd been –"

But he was laughing at her and she stopped speaking, tightening her grip on her bag helplessly. How she disliked him when he did that!

"You'd make a good detective, do you know that? There's a clever girl, putting two and two together. The only trouble with people like you is that you invariably get it to make five when you do. So I went out for a perfectly innocent stroll, and just because you see a telephone kiosk a distance away, you have me going there. Now why? I'm a man who wakes early. It was a pleasant morning, so I did what anyone would do on their last morning in a place, I went for a little walk. Your imagination is working overtime, my child –"

"I'm not your child," she snapped. "Don't be so stupidly patronising."

"Ouch! Don't the sharp edges hurt?"

She knew she shouldn't have asked the second she said it, but then it was too late.

"On what?"

"On your tongue. For such a young woman – how old are you? – nineteen? –"

"That's none of your business," she snapped.

"You have a remarkably sharp tongue," he went on as if she had not interrupted. "Tell me why, I'd like to know. I mean, wouldn't it be easier to be nice to everybody, or wouldn't you like to try that?"

"Coming from you, that's *good*. You can be insufferably arrogant without even trying –"

"Was I arrogant with Aunt Sofia? Esko – Liisa? The people at the party?" he demanded. "Go on, answer me. Have you seen or heard me being arrogant – as *you* call it – with anyone we've met over this weekend?"

"You've certainly thrown your weight about with me –" she began, because there was really no answer to his question, except the one she was not prepared to give.

"I'm not talking about you now, I'm talking about everyone else, and you can't answer me. Of course I've thrown my weight about, as you so childishly put it, with you, because damn me, you get my dander up the minute you open your mouth, with your snooty little 'I'm somebody important, so watch it' ways." He gave her a hard level glance from his position at the controls. "It took me all my self-control to stop from giving you

84

the damned good spanking you deserve in your bedroom yesterday – so just think yourself lucky. You'd not have been sitting so comfortably now if I had, I promise you that." And he turned back to look at the rows of dials as if that was of far more interest.

"If that so-called kiss was instead of the spanking, then I can tell you which I would have preferred," retorted Eve. "Believe me, you provide no competition to Casanova." She managed a little laugh. "Heavens, you call *that* a kiss!"

"I've had no complaints in the past," and he smiled. "So if you're trying to make me feel unsure of myself, don't bother, I prefer the opinions of experts in some matters, and you, Eve, are a non-starter."

It was precisely what she had been attempting, knowing that laughter is the surest way to make a man doubt his ability as a lover – but he had swiftly turned the tables on her. To be called a non-starter, by someone as insufferable as him, was the last straw.

"I don't want to speak to you," she said stiffly, fighting down sheer temper.

"Good. That suits me. I can concentrate on flying this plane – which, as you've reminded me several times, is what I've been hired to do. However, I would like to point out that there's a flask of Aunt Sofia's excellent coffee beside me, and you may have some when you wish."

Eve turned her head away without deigning to reply. And neither of them spoke for the next half hour or so. Then, suddenly, the sky grew dark and heavy, and within seconds of that warning they were in the middle of a rainstorm. She looked at him, then at the sheets of water cascading down the outside of the cabin, making them appear to be submerged in the centre of a waterfall. A little shiver of fear, a mere frisson, touched her spine. It was all happening so suddenly, and yet he appeared quite unmoved by it, his hands, large, capable, suntanned hands, were steady on the controls, even though the land beneath them was no more than a grey-green washed-out blur. And then the plane juddered, and she saw his frown, his sudden move towards a switch. Fear overrode her animosity.

"What is it?" she said.

He didn't look at her. He was busy concentrating. "I don't know," he said. "You needn't worry. We're not going to crash or anything, I promise you that. But something is playing havoc with the controls. The compass is going mad. Don't talk – just fasten your belt – and don't worry."

And strangely, with his words, the fear vanished. Eve fastened her seat belt and sat very still. She knew the value of silence at times of crisis, knew too that Garth was a skilled pilot. He had said they were not going to crash, and she believed him. It began to be like a strange kind of dream, those next few minutes as he circled – at least it felt as if they were circling – lower and lower, and the juddering became a rumble, as if the very framework of the aircraft was going to be torn apart with the rain – and then Garth said, in a taut voice: "Hold tight, Eve. We're going to land."

It was pitch darkness. Eerie, because it was day. But

they were safe, on water, the plane being rocked by the rain, buffeted by the wind outside. Eve shivered, and he said: "Are you cold?"

"No, not really. Where – where are we?" Just for a second, her voice faltered.

He took a deep, deep breath. It was as if he was making some inward decision. Eve could sense it, almost like vibrations in the small cabin. "I haven't the faintest idea," he said, and then he picked up the flask of coffee and, unscrewing the top, poured some out. "You'd better drink this," he said, almost gently for him, "before I tell you the bad news."

Eve took the small beaker from him. There was something, something . . .

"What is it?" she said calmly, and lifted her chin.

"The engine's completely dead." It was said in such a matter-of-fact tone that at first it didn't register. Then it did, and she looked sharply at him.

"I didn't understand. It was all right minutes ago – or we wouldn't have landed as we did –"

"That landing took all my skill – and the last remnants of the engine's power. I know, I've just been examining instruments as well as I can in this strange light – and I can tell you that there's less energy underneath this instrument panel than in my cigarette lighter."

She had seen his face, dimly, sensed the movements of his hands in the first startling moments after they settled, but none of it had really registered because the sense of relief had been too great to allow any other feelings. "Then what do we do?" she asked.

"You're a cool one, aren't you? Some girls would have burst into tears by now, and –"

"I'm not 'some girls,' I'm me." she met the shadowy grey glance with equanimity. "I don't panic – or burst into tears at the slightest provocation. But I would like to know what we're going to do. We certainly can't sit here all day, can we?"

"We're going to find somewhere to prepare some food for a start – I'm starving. Then, when we've got shelter, we'll think it over. Do you want to wait here while I scout round?"

"I'll do what you suggest," she answered.

"Then wait here. I'll be back as soon as I can." He stood up and went to the rear of the plane, moving cautiously in the gloom. The relentless hammering of heavy rain on the outer surface of the plane was becoming almost a soothing sound – but Eve knew it would not be pleasant to be in it. He wore a heavy oilskin and his wellingtons when he returned. But it wasn't this which riveted Eve's attention. It was the rifle he carried.

He held it up. "Bears," he remarked succinctly, and moved towards the door.

Eve could only repeat the word. "Bears?" she said.

"Mmm, probably won't see one, but –" and he grinned tightly, "I'd rather not wait until we're in touching distance before wishing I'd taken a rifle. I don't need to tell you to stay here, do I?" and without waiting for an answer, he opened the door, swung himself down, and closed it shut after him. The silence after his departure hung about her like a mist. And the implications of what had happened were just beginning to sink in. She knew she must not blame him, and yet – and yet they were here, stuck possibly for hours, until help arrived. Eve took a deep breath. Her first instinct had been right. She had disliked him. She hadn't known he was trouble – not then. But she did now. On no account must she let her feelings show. He would enjoy that; he would take pleasure from seeing her dismayed and angry. It appeared as if the parting words at Helsinki might have to wait a while longer. But oh, how rich and satisfying they would be when she did actually get there.

She looked at her watch. Nearly half an hour had passed. The rain was dying away, and with its going came a little light. The wind too was lessening, silence and stillness taking over from the noise and movement of the elements. And with them came loneliness. She was completely alone in an alien world. Garth could have been a million miles away. Suppose that a bear came to the door. Suppose . . .

But that was ridiculous. Eve leaned over to look out, to see where they actually were. She wished, a moment later, that she hadn't. They were right at the edge of the lake, and the lack of light was as much due to the departing rain as to the high trees towering all around, hiding the sky. The water was grey and grim, stiller now, and the earth surrounding it, before the trees began, was black, black as pitch. And not a bird or a creature moved. A fancy took hold of her. What if he had seen someone – perhaps a hunter, with a plane, and just gone, leaving her to her fate? It was a brief notion, lasting only a few seconds before it vanished, swallowed by reason. Why leave a perfectly good plane – and his clothes – even if he did dislike her? She smiled at the absurdness of the idea, but the aftertaste lingered, and she found herself counting slowly. When she reached a hundred, he'd be back. One – two – three – four –

"Eve?" The door opening, his voice, matter-of-fact, unconcerned. "It's nearly stopped, but grab a mac and wellingtons anyway. And – oh yes – pass me down the box of food, will you? Save me getting in." Relief at hearing him was swiftly followed by annoyance at his complete taking over, again, as if he was in charge –

"Come on, we've not got all day. I'm starving even if you're not –"

"I'm coming." Now was not the time for any arguments. She was hungry herself, and cold, not just an ordinary coldness, but a bone-biting, marrow-aching one, and anything warm would be welcome, and she would do what she was told, because if he wanted that box of food it must mean he had found a place to shelter – and to eat. She passed him the box and he said: "The mac's behind you – and the wellies. I'll dump this on the ground and come back for you."

The water was so shallow where he had landed that his help wasn't necessary, merely a strong arm to guide her downwards. Splashing, stumbling, shivering, she followed him into the thick dark trees, and wondered to herself, Where the hell are we going?

The first surprise was the cabin in the clearing. The

second surprise came when he opened the door and they went in. A crackling wood fire burnt merrily in the open fireplace, showering red sparks up the chimney. The sight was such that she immediately felt better. "Oh," she said. "*Oh!* warmth –" and she went and knelt in front of it, holding her hands up, basking in the yellow flames.

"That's why I took so long," Garth said, putting down the box, taking off his oilskin, coming over to crouch beside her. "It took me a while to find this place, and when I did I built a fire immediately."

"But – what if the owners –" she faltered. There was something about his face, some expression of hidden laughter, of *knowing* something that she didn't.

"Don't you know?" he asked. "Have you *forgotten?*"

"Forgotten what?" But some memory was there, tantalizingly at the very back of her consciousness.

"The *autiotupa* – the wilderness huts I was telling you about. What do you think this is?"

"This is one of them?" But she didn't need to ask really, she knew now. Slowly she looked around her, taking it all in, realizing what he meant. Spartan was the word that sprang immediately to her mind. There was a table, and two benches, and the open fireplace set in a stone wall. The other three walls were of smooth pine logs, two with a small window, the last, the one behind them, with the door. And beside the fireplace, but not too near, was a raised wooden platform about six feet wide. And that was it.

She took a deep breath. "Yes. Yes, I see. And people stay here – they actually sleep in these?" She couldn't hide the horror she felt at the primitive air of it all.

"I have, several times," he raised a gently mocking eyebrow. "Not in this one, of course, but they're all pretty much alike, built to an almost standard design. That –" he pointed to the platform, "is to sleep on – keeps you off the draughty floor." He grinned. "And there's a table, a bench – what more could one ask?"

"You don't want me to answer that, do you?" Eve said sweetly. "And where's the bathroom, for heaven's sake?"

"Oh, forgive me!" he clapped his hand to his mouth in mock dismay. "I forgot to have one installed for you."

"Don't be sarcastic," she said. She was beginning to thaw out now, and feeling fractionally better, but even hungrier. "Please can we eat – and then see about getting out of here?"

He stood up and turned away as she spoke, so that she couldn't see his face. Then he was busy at the table, taking tins and packets from the carton, and his tone was deceptively casual as he said:

"It might not be quite that easy, I'm afraid."

She jumped up and went over to him. "What do you mean?"

He shrugged. "I'll have a look at the engine as soon as we've had a meal, but it seemed very dead to me."

"And if it is, you have a radio, don't you? I saw it."

"Everything's dead, not just the engine. That too."

And then it began to sink in. Only gradually, of

course. The sheer improbability of it all was too much to grasp in a few moments. I must keep calm, Eve thought; I *must* keep very calm. "What," she said, very slowly and clearly, "are you trying to tell me?"

"I would have thought it was obvious. We may have to spend the night here."

She burst out laughing. "You must be joking! *Me* stay here with *you*? You're mad!"

"And I'll tell you something else too, miss," he said, "while we're on the subject. We're both going to have to sleep together on that platform, because I'm not freezing on the floor for you or anybody, and I'm quite sure you won't want to either."

She looked across at the platform. It was like a miniature stage. And about the size of a good double bed, no more. "I'd rather sleep on the plane," she said flatly, "than here with you. I've heard some yarns in my time, but you take the biscuit –"

"And what precisely do you mean by that crack?" He paused in the act of opening a tin of soup. He hadn't even bothered to ask what she would like to eat.

"I shouldn't need to spell it out, should I?" she responded tartly. "You're a man – or so I've been led to believe –"

"Well, yes, I'm sure I am," he cut in, "but we might as well get one thing perfectly straight here and now. And this may come as quite a shock to you, because it's obvious from the way you behave that you're used to everyone fawning over you and making you the centre of attention, but here's the surprise – *I* don't fancy you, adore you *or* lust after you. My manly heart does not leap in my bosom at the sight of you, nor do you send my pulse rate or temperature up in the slightest. In short, and I'm sorry to be so brutally frank because I'm sure you're not used to it, you're as safe here with me as you would be with Aunt Sofia – probably safer in fact, because I bet she can't fight off bears –"

"You are the most insulting *beast* –" Eve began, her cheeks flaring into red at his words.

"Ah, ah, temper! I've told you before about it. If you want to eat, just behave yourself, or you can get your own –"

"It would be a pleasure," she grated, and he handed her the tin-opener and turned away towards the fire. Eve looked at the metal contraption in her hand. On the rare occasions that she had actually had to open a tin of something herself, there had been an electric wall-opener to do it. This didn't look even remotely like anything to do with tin-opening. It could possibly have been an instrument for Boy Scouts to dash around getting stones out of horses' hooves with; it might conceivably be used for scratching one's name on a tree – but that was all.

She looked across to where Garth had transferred the contents of the soup tin into a pannikin which he was now delicately balancing at the front of the fire, using the empty tin for partial support. Eve's stomach protested as the first wisps of steam rose gently. "I can't use this *thing*," she said.

"Why not?" He didn't turn at first. Not until he was satisfied the little pan would not fall. Then he rose. "Are you helpless or something?"

"You did it deliberately," she accused him. "You need practice using this kind of thing –"

"You were throwing your weight about, remember? Not me. You asked for it. You got it. Now do you want to share the soup and some crackers or not?" And he opened a packet of small cracker-like biscuits and looked up at her. "Don't try and treat me like one of your servants. Unless you want to see me get really mad, that is, and I don't think you'd like that, quite honestly."

Eve sat down, She was too hungry to care any more. "Yes, please," she said. She was exhausted too. A mixture of delayed shock and dismay at this surprising new situation, she imagined, but whatever the cause, her legs wouldn't support her any more. And, absurdly, she felt like bursting into tears, and that she would *never* do. Not in front of *him*.

"That's better." He dug into the box again and produced two metal plates and spoons. "Just remember your manners and you'll do fine. You'll find me very helpful when I'm treated right – hired help though I may be." And he turned away to the fire and carried back the soup and poured it into the plates.

It was good, it was oh, so very good. Eve had not realized just how starving she really was until she actually tasted the rich chunky mixture of vegetables and meat in rich broth. His voice was an intrusion.

"Coffee?" he said.

"Please." And then she saw that he had put the flask in the box too – presumably when he had been to get his oilskin and wellingtons on. Almost as if he had

95

known in advance they would be coming here to eat. She dismissed the brief thought as he poured out hot coffee into a beaker. Just one. "Where's your cup?" she asked.

"I'll drink after you. There's another in the plane somewhere – plus, if I can find it, some more food and coffee. We'll go back and collect our luggage when you've finished."

There didn't seem to be anything more to say. Not for the moment anyway. Eve felt strength and warmth returning to her limbs as she finished the thick broth, and drank the hot coffee. She was even able to watch him with a kind of quiet calm as he poured out his own drink from the flask, and lit a cheroot. There was one thing she could hardly refuse to admit privately to herself. He was cool, relaxed and quite at home. and she knew then that that was how he would be in any situation, however bizarre. For this was – a quiet peaceful flight from Rovaniemi to Helsinki rudely broken by a hectic sequence of events, still too close to be thought about coherently; a sudden violent rainstorm, the plane's instruments going haywire; a landing on a lake in virtual darkness – the danger of bears – and now *this*. This being a meal eaten in a wilderness hut, beside a blazing fire, and sitting across a crude wooden table from a man she disliked – and with the awful prospect of having to spend the coming hours of darkness alone with him. Entirely alone. She thought about that last fact for a few moments as she watched him finish his coffee.

He gave her a brief tight smile and stood up. "Ready?" he asked.

"For what?" For a second she was confused. .

"Why, to return to the plane, of course. Then you can see for yourself that I'm not lying when I say that everything is dead –"

"I'd hardly know anyway; would I?" she retorted coolly. "I don't know the first thing about planes."

He raised an amused eyebrow. "Then you can come back to help me carry stuff," he answered with infuriating calm. "Will that do you? Tell me, do you still have lingering doubts about my intentions? Because if so –"

She jumped to her feet. "Don't be ridiculous! I –"

"Because," he cut in, voice hard enough to stop hers in its tracks, "I'm fast getting weary of assuring you about *that*. This is the last sort of place I'd plan on for a seduction, I promise you –"

"Can we change the subject?" she said.

"Certainly. What do you want to talk about? Luggage? The state of the world? The Common Market?"

"Luggage will do for a start. Are we fetching it all back here?"

"It might be safer. You never know what you'll need, and it'll be no fun trekking back after dark. Have you any warm clothes?"

"Yes, but –" she faltered.

"It gets very cold here at night. Very cold. As you will no doubt discover. We're not in a cosy centrally heated house now, you know. We only have the fire to rely on, and that will die down during the night unless you keep stoking it up. When I sleep, I sleep, so to go to bed tonight, you put on all your warmest togs and you should be all right." He paused, flicked the finished cheroot at the fire where it vanished into the yellow flames without trace, then said almost hesitantly: "Do you want the good news or the bad news?"

It sounded like the beginning of a corny joke, but she didn't really find much to laugh at in his expression. There seemed to be a faint trace of that dark hidden amusement in his eyes, and somehow, that never boded good for her.

Eve took a deep breath. "Go on," she said cautiously. "What is it?"

"I've only got one sleeping bag," he said, and now his face was carefully expressionless. She should have known what was coming next. She really should have known.

"But it's big enough for two," he added.

Eve turned away. She didn't want him to see her face. How she hated him! "Don't worry," she said. "It's all yours." And she went to put on her oilskin. "I'll manage."

"I knew you'd say that," he answered, and opened the door to a gust of wind and a flurry of rain, which even as they watched, deepened to a heavy downpour. She walked out into it with upturned face. The weather matched her mood. Just one question now in her mind. Could things really get worse than they already were? It didn't seem possible.

CHAPTER SEVEN

THE second journey back to their shelter was even worse than the first. For then there had been faint hope of a pleasant surprise, perhaps even of people. Now she knew what to expect – a spartan hut, its only bright spot a good fire. Eve followed Garth, her wellingtoned feet squelching in his tracks as she strove to keep up with his longer strides. He made no concessions to her in the matter of speed. Even though he carried cases, and the rifle slung over his shoulder, he moved quickly. Eve carried another boxful of food and small items that he had flung in from the plane. And then they had left it, without a backward glance. So, thought Eve, I accept the fact that we're here for the night. But when morning comes – what then? And so important was the question that they were scarcely inside the door before she asked it.

Garth put the cases, his own duffel bag, a large rolled-up bundle, and the rifle, down by the door, and began to pull off his shiny oilskins. "We set off walking," he said. "To try and get our bearings for a start, but more important, to find people. I said 'we', but I'll go alone, of course, if you don't feel up to it."

"I want to come with you," she said hastily. "I'm not staying here alone."

He frowned. "You'd be quite safe, I promise you. You can barricade the door – if you're frightened of

99

bears. But they don't actually go searching people out, you know, not unless they're starving, and that would be highly unlikely at this time of year –"

"I'd rather come." She had a horror of being left completely alone – there.

"It won't be easy. We may have to walk miles and miles in pouring rain –"

"Please," she said. "I don't care."

He shrugged. "Okay. Now let's get unloaded. Firstly, that box you carried." He went to where she had put it on the table. "I've brought a compass, amongst other things. We'll need that in the morning." He took out a small pouch and laid it carefully on the table. "I suggest you dig in your cases and find a couple of warm sweaters, and an extra pair of trousers. Got any socks?"

"No. Just tights."

"Hmm. Well, if you can bear to wear anything of mine, I'll lend you a spare pair. They are clean," he added dryly. Eve bit her underlip, suddenly and quite uncharacteristically unsure of herself.

"Thank you," she said.

"You're welcome." She couldn't tell if there was sarcasm in his voice. She didn't want to find out. She went and knelt by one case and unlocked it to reveal her clothes neatly folded. With a little sigh she felt underneath the top layer for a thick blue sweater, one she nearly hadn't bothered to bring, but had added as an afterthought. After that she lifted out a dark pair of trousers and took both items over for his inspection.

He spared them a brief glance. "They'll do," he said.

"Put them near the fire to warm." It was much easier just to do as he said without arguing, she was already beginning to find that out; so she did as she was told. She watched him go over to the rolled-up bundle by the door. And then she realized what it was. He carefully unrolled the sleeping bag on to the broad platform by the fireplace. It was of thick padded nylon, orange and blue squares, eye-blinkingly vivid.

"It can be seen from a great height," he said, almost gently. Eve swallowed the instant retort that almost sprang to her lips: why don't we stick it on the roof of the plane then? and said instead: "I see."

It was nearly six o'clock. Soon it would be dark, although the rain was making it so already. And she was beginning to feel hungry again. Hardly surprising, considering the time. "I'm hungry," she said, not caring if he was scornful – quite prepared to discover how that awful tin-opening contraption worked if he mocked her again. But he didn't.

" So am I," he agreed. "We only had soup before, and that trek to the plane and back gives me an appetite. Okay, we'll eat – not just soup and crackers this time, but a proper meal. It's rumoured that I'm a fair chef – in certain circles. I'm also, as I have no intention of forgetting, supposed to be looking after you. So will you leave it all to me?" and he looked at her enquiringly, no trace of the usual dark mockery about his face, nothing save what seemed to be a polite concern.

" Yes," she said promptly, "I'll leave it to you."

He nodded. "Fine. Now if you want to – er – wash

and brush up, I suggest you put on your mac and go outside. There's a primitive kind of rain barrel at the back. You can wash your face in that. As for the – ahem – bathroom – well, I'm afraid –" he stopped, and once again, it seemed that he might be fighting back laughter.

"All right," said Eve, keeping her voice calm with an effort, "you don't need to describe it in detail, I get the picture." And she picked up her oilskin and went to the door. The rain fell in torrents, but strangely enough, she was past worrying about it. Everything was ghastly, the whole situation. She had been mad to come. She should have stayed at home. What could be worse? Perhaps a rampaging bear? She shrugged to herself, opened the door, and went out. Right into a huge puddle.

Dignity is difficult when you are covered with mud, but she managed. When she returned to the wilderness hut, Eve stood just inside the door, waiting for his laughter, ready to wither him with a glance if he said one single word – but he was too engrossed in his task at the fireplace to even look round.

"Won't be long," he said. "Get your mac off. Perhaps you'll clear a space at the table?" He wasn't asking – he was telling her. And the rather delicious aroma of cooking meat was making her feel faint. She peeled off the soaking oilskin, surveyed her mud-covered knees, shrugged, and bent to remove her wellingtons. A few minutes later, sitting at the table with her feet encased in her warm slippers, she began to

102

feel a little better. Not much, but just a little. And it was enough for now.

"There are three candles in that box you carried," he said. "Get one out and light it. There's a metal tin that does as candle-holder – can you see it?"

She was rummaging in the box, surprised at the variety of items within it, a wild, stupid suspicion growing in her mind ... "You seem to be well prepared," she said eventually, her tone very casual.

"Oh, I am. I've told you before, I've spent days in these places in the past. So now I never travel without everything I need for comfort. Don't worry, you'll be well looked after here."

It was not quite what she meant. A full meaningful silence hung in the air for a few moments after his words. And Garth slowly straightened up from the fire and turned to her. "Say it," he suggested gently. "Get it off your chest – whatever it is."

She shook her head. "Nothing."

"Oh yes, there damn well is!" He crossed to the table. "Spit it out!"

"All right, I will!" Defiance flared. He couldn't be much worse than he already was. "It seems remarkably as though – as though you'd planned all this in advance – as if –" the words refused to come out. They were too outlandish, too *horrific* to express.

"Go *on*," he urged, and she was frightened of the dark strength in his face.

"Have you kidnapped me?" she burst out – and braced herself for him to strike her, flinching almost visibly as she saw his face change. It changed all right –

but not to unleashed anger. To sheer amusement. To laughter.

When he could speak, he gasped: "Kidnapped? *Me* – kidnap – *you*! I don't think I've laughed so much for ages." Then he sobered slightly. "Is that really what you thought?"

The relief was enormous. There was no pretence in his laughter. She shook her head. "It's happened before. And you know I'm wealthy. You must know that."

He sat down. "Yes, I do know that. It must be obvious to everyone you meet, Eve. But I promise you I'm no kidnapper. Just think about it for a moment. Do you think I'd let all those people – Esko – Liisa – Aunt Sofia – know I'd taken you off in a plane if I was? Surely the idea is for an abductor to remain unknown? Everyone knows me. And anyway, just give me one good reason why I should. No, I'll tell you. Money. That's the reason, always. But I don't need money. I have all I need, or ever will. Does that surprise you?"

She could look up to meet his eyes. The feeling of humiliation was a new one to Eve. "Everyone wants more money," she said flatly.

He grinned briefly. "Perhaps among *your* kind of friends. I'm not your kind of person, though, thank God. I'm *me*. I got my values sorted out a long time ago."

"What you're trying to say is that you'd prefer to stay here for a holiday rather than at some comfortable hotel?" She was beginning to feel angry. Was there no way of beating him?

104

"In a word – yes."

"I don't believe you."

"I can well imagine that! But as we're speaking so frankly I'll be blunt as well. Just precisely how happy are you, Eve?"

" I don't know what you mean!" This defensively.

"You do, you know. Are you happy, I asked – but I didn't need to, because I know the answer already. You're not. You're discontented and bored, which is why you travel around searching for something – I'll bet you don't even know what it is yourself –"

"Don't talk so stupid!" she snapped.

"See what I mean? You start these things, but when they don't go the way you want, you accuse me of being stupid. I'm happy in my life. I'm not searching for anything out of life, I've found it. I'm satisfied with what I'm doing –"

"Can't we eat?" she cut in. "I'm hungry – or I was. If you keep on insulting me and coming out with your home spun bits of philosophy I shall lose my appetite."

"Or in other words – shut up, Garth. Okay, we'll eat. And any time you want to discuss the meaning of life again, just let me know."

"There won't be time," she said, and smiled. "We'll be away from here soon, and I'll be rid of you."

He stood up. "You express yourself so clearly, dear Eve. That's one thing I like about you. You don't mince words." But he was amused again, not laughing, but not far from it.

"If I were a man," she burst out, knowing she really

shouldn't, but stung by that air of calm of his, "I'd punch you on the nose!"

He raised his eyebrows in mock horror. "Heavens to Betsy! That's not very ladylike. I must be thankful you're not a man, then. I don't like fighting."

"No?" She managed to inject utter disbelief into one word.

"No. People who seek out fights are generally immature. You've only got to watch the News and read the papers to see that."

"Immature – or cowards," she said softly.

"And if you're hoping to rile me with a few well chosen taunts, you won't succeed," he said, quite gently for him. "You really should have learned that by now. If you wish to think me a coward, I don't really care. Not one bit. So – now we'll eat. The food's ready." And he turned away from her. She knew she should not have said what she had. There had been nothing about him to suggest cowardice, or even mild panic, in all that had happened since leaving Rovaniemi. Quite the reverse. In those few bad minutes when it seemed anything might happen during the rainstorm, he had been like a man of steel, completely cool and resourceful.

Eve swallowed hard, and before thinking too much about it, said: "I shouldn't have said that. I'm sorry."

He was carrying steaming pans towards the table. He put them down and looked at her. Then he smiled. "That's all right. You're learning."

His words came back to her later, much later, when it
106.

was dark, and the wind howled, and the rain lashed ceaselessly down outside, and she was alone. Sitting on the bench by the fire, Eve looked into the glowing, sparking logs, and saw again his face as he had said those two words: "You're learning." There had been something in the way he said them, some significance which had escaped her at the time. So subtle that even now she wasn't sure, but she shivered slightly as she regarded the crackling yellow flames. He was no ordinary man. Just a few minutes previously he had picked up his oilskin and said to her: "I suggest you get yourself togged up for the night. I'll not be long." And then he had thrown a pair of socks to her from his duffel bag, and gone out.

She didn't argue. She pulled on the warm dark trews and the extra sweater. Now she bent to put on the socks, and the door crashed open and he came in again, in a blast of icy air and damp.

"It's getting worse if anything," he said. "Ready for bed? Good. Now, are we going to have lots of silly arguments about the sleeping bag or do we save time by agreeing to share it in a strictly impersonal way?"

He had told her that she didn't mince words. Eve breathed deeply and stood up. Neither did he. "I can't," she answered. "It's as simple as that. I just can't. Don't you see?"

"Under normal circumstances – yes," he answered. "But these are not normal circumstances. It's simply a matter of keeping warm. I can't make you believe me when I say you're perfectly safe, I appreciate that. I just don't know how to put it any more clearly. But let me say one thing. We're miles from anywhere, quite alone, and we've been here for hours. If I had had any evil intentions I'd have been perfectly able to have carried them out before now. As it is, I'm very tired. I shall be asleep in a couple of minutes, I promise you that." He shrugged. "That's all. If you can't accept that – there's only one thing more to say. If you really are so frightened of me, I'll sleep on the damned table – okay?"

It was his last words that did it. He was not being flippant now, simply stating facts. And he did look tired. Eve nodded. "All right," she said, "I believe you."

"Okay. In you get. I'll stoke up the fire first, though it will have died out by morning anyway."

The sleeping bag was extraordinarily warm. She had never been in one before, let alone tried to sleep, but as she slid into the soft padded nylon, wriggling her toes down, Eve swallowed her last vestige of pride. Too late to back out now. She lay back on the air pillow and looked warily at the one beside her. It was terribly close. She turned away, towards the wall, and tried to relax. It was quite impossible, of course. Her body tensed for his arrival, was stiff and taut. She closed her eyes, but she knew she would never get to sleep.

There were the faint sounds as he moved around the hut, building up the logs on the fire from the neat pile beside it, checking that the door was secured against the elements, moving a tin plate with a small chink, and then, finally, blowing out the candle. The eerie shadows from the fire danced on the ceiling as Eve

108

peeped upwards. And then his feet padding across the floor – towards her.

Then he was in beside her, behind her, and she heard him zip up the cover. His breath was soft upon her neck as he said quietly: "You can relax now, Eve. Good night."

"Good night," a muffled whisper from her. Tense, unmoving, she lay, counting her breathing in an effort to calm herself. Minutes passed. She could feel the warmth of his body, as he must surely be able to from hers. And his breathing deepened, became slower – and she knew that he was asleep. Gradually the tension slipped away from her, and although she tried to keep her eyes open they grew heavier and heavier, the warmth swallowed her up. Incredible softness and comfort fought a winning battle with her own inner struggle, and with a little sigh, she fell asleep.

When she awoke she didn't know where she was – worse, she didn't know this strange sleeping man lying so close to her – and she started in alarm, then, as memory flooded back, lay still again. It was pitch darkness, both inside and outside, and the rain was a distant pattering on the roof, no more. They must have both turned over in their sleep, for her back was to the wall now, and she lay behind Garth. The air on her face was cold. Perhaps that was what had awoken her. But the rest of her, from the neck downwards, was in a cocoon of warmth. She wondered what time it was, but dared not move to try and see her watch. Her elbow, she realized suddenly, was digging into his back, and very gently she eased it away, then froze as he muttered: "Whassa – um?" still sleeping, not awake.

She held her breath, fearful he should waken fully, then relaxed as his murmur died away, his breathing slowed again. How foolish she had been even to consider not believing him. She should have accepted what he said instead of fighting it, causing a great fuss, showing herself to be quite immature. So much so that in the end he had offered to sleep on the table. And she knew he would have done so. Then they would both have been cold, especially him. She sighed a little sigh, more in sadness than anything else. In a way she had attempted to judge him by John and Neil, and she should not have done. There was a world of difference between Garth and them, in so many ways. Even allowing for the fact that both other men each loved her in their own way, and Garth most definitely did not, their behaviour would have been vastly different if either had had to spend the night alone with her.

She moved very slightly, because one of his legs was on hers, and it had gone dead – and he suddenly came awake and said: "What is it?"

"I'm sorry," she said quickly. "My leg – I was just easing it –"

"Okay. Is that better?"

"Yes. Thanks." She couldn't help it. She had gone tense again.

"Want a coffee?"

"A coffee?" she repeated foolishly.

"Yes. It must be nearly morning and I'm going to see

if there's any life left in the fire. If there is I'll heat some water."

"Yes, please," she said, more promptly this time.

"Right. Don't move. I'll manage." And silently he unzipped himself and slid out of the sleeping bag. Bliss! She could move, and stretch herself freely. The candle flickered and cast a pale yellow light and he said: "It's nearly five." Eve sat up and stretched wide her arms. Surprisingly she had slept well. She watched him moving round the room, kneeling at the hearth, pushing bits of paper into dying embers to coax it into life, and she sat there hugging her knees, and suddenly she had an incredible thought. Just for a second it lasted, but it was: I can almost know what he means about these huts. She had never imagined she would, but the idea lingered, because there was a certain atmosphere about the place, hard to define, virtually impossible to put into words, but it was there. It was a *comfortable* feeling. And the idea of drinking a cup of coffee in that half light, by a flickering fire, was something that appealed more with each moment that passed.

"Can I help you?" she asked.

"No, I'll manage. This fire will be going again in a few minutes. Then I'll go and fetch water from outside. Did you sleep well?"

"Yes, thanks. Did you?"

"Yes. I always do."

"You were asleep within minutes," she said, not understanding how or why they could be having this pleasant conversation without any of the usual undertones of aggression and conflict.

111

"I'm sure I was. Which must have enabled you to relax, I imagine. You were tensed up like a coiled spring when I got in. So now do you believe me?" He wasn't mocking her, it was still pleasant and relaxed, the barriers down.

Eve nodded. "Yes."

"Good. That makes life easier all round, doesn't it?"

"You don't have to sound so bossy," she said, but not sharply, just as a comment.

Garth laughed. "Okay, okay, sorry. I'd have been just the same as you if I were a girl –" he paused, then added: "I imagine so anyway."

"You would have been if you'd met some of the men I know," she said. She didn't know why she was speaking thus to him. Perhaps it was the time of night, when she was still not far enough from sleep to be on guard.

He nodded. "Ah, yes, you have a point there. I'm sorry about that. Some men can be swine. Just as long as you remember not to judge us all by the same standards, because we're not all alike." He stood up and surveyed his handiwork, the yellow flames beginning to crackle anew. "That'll do. It'll soon be going nicely. I'll go for the water, then you'll be drinking a nice cup of Garth Seton's special coffee in about five minutes."

She watched him go out. Watched him, and thought: sometimes he can be quite human – almost – nice. And that was a ridiculous notion to have. I must be still half asleep, she told herself severely.

He knew how to make coffee, no doubt about that.

Eve sipped the steaming hot liquid and sighed gratefully. "Mmm, lovely."

"Do you mind if I go and have a scout round?"

Alarm flared in her. "Now? In the dark?"

"I can find my way better, believe it or not. I wouldn't go far. Just try and get a bearing on where we are – and see if we're near civilization."

She swallowed hard. The obvious thing was to say yes. After all, she was perfectly safe, and could bolt the door after him. But suppose he didn't return? Suppose . . .

"We'll leave it until later if you like. It's just that I know I won't sleep again now, and I thought it would give you a rest in peace."

It was no use. She already knew what he thought of her, in many different ways. And she had virtually accused him of being a coward the previous evening. It would be ironic if she were now to act like a timid little girl.

"Of course. I'll have another little sleep."

He finished his coffee. "Right. Do you want to bolt the door after me?"

"Yes, if you don't mind."

"I don't. It's just that I'll wake you up when I return."

"I doubt if I'll sleep anyway."

But she did, and the thunderous knocking on the door roused her from a very vivid dream about sleeping in a strange hotel, high in the trees.

"Just a minute." She ran across the room, tousle-haired, opened the door and rubbed the sleep from her

113

eyes. Garth stood there, wearing his lumberjacket – it had stopped raining – jeans, wellingtons, Beatle cap on the back of his head, and carrying his rifle in one hand and a very dead bird in the other. Eve's eyes widened. "What's that?"

"A grouse. Our breakfast – and maybe dinner too."

"You *shot* it?" She couldn't help the grimace of distaste.

"Yes. And before you pull any more faces, I don't shoot for sport – only for food. And don't tell me you've never been hunting." And he walked in. The truce, or whatever it had been, was over.

"Of course I haven't," she flared back. "I suppose you have?"

"Don't be ridiculous. I just told you, I don't kill for fun. I shot this on the way back from my scouting foray because for one thing it practically fell out of a tree on to my rifle – we'd probably find it died of old age anyway if we did a post-mortem – and for the second thing –" and here he hesitated, laid the bird on the table, and turned towards Eve, "the news about our situation isn't very good, I'm afraid –"

"What – what do you mean?" she breathed. There was something rather frightening about his face.

"I've been for miles. I've cut a circle round this place, I've combed it – and I've listened for any sounds of civilization. I've not seen or heard a single thing anywhere. We're completely and utterly lost."

CHAPTER EIGHT

"But – but we can't be! What are we going to do?" Eve felt an unbearable panic rising within her. It was a stifling sensation, horrible, shadowy, filling her body and mind, making her go weak. This couldn't be happening. It *could not*. But it was. It was like a nightmare coming to life. And then she saw that he was watching her, coolly, appraisingly. Swift anger rose to replace the panic. But before she could speak, he said:

"You're terrified. Why?"

"Why? *Why?* Why do you *think*? You – you stand there, calmly telling me we're completely lost, and expect me not to be frightened –"

"It doesn't mean we're here for ever. Is that what you thought? It just means it might take us a little longer to find our way back to civilization."

"How?"

He pulled up a chair, his air of infuriating calm upsetting her as much as anything else. "Not by rushing round bleating like sheep, that's for sure." He pulled out a cheroot and lit it. She felt like striking it from his hand. She had to clench her hands tightly to stop herself. And he looked up, and said:

"Sit down, Eve."

"No!"

"*Sit down.*" The eyes were steel, his face equally hard. She sat down. "That's better. Right. I've got a map of Finland in my duffel bag. We'll eat first and then have a good look at it. First of all, though, we'll have another cup of coffee. Okay?"

She shrugged. "Why ask me? You're the one giving the orders round here."

He shook his head gently. "Oh dear, oh dear! Your temper is showing, little girl. I'm not going to force you to drink coffee – or to eat breakfast, for that matter. Talking of which, we'll have the grouse for lunch – I don't suppose you know how to prepare one, do you?"

"No, I don't." It was an effort to answer him.

"Well, it's never too late to learn, I always say. So I'll show you afterwards."

"Will you? Why don't you do it yourself, if you're so clever?" she retorted. "I'm supposed to be on holiday, not learning woodcraft with some idiot who doesn't even know where he is." She could barely sit still. Her voice was trembling with the effort to speak at all.

Garth stood up and went to the hearth without speaking. He put on a couple of logs and then the pan of water. Then he turned round, slowly, calmly. She should have been warned, should have noticed the leashed strength and force of his movements, the tight control, but she was too angry herself to heed the warning signs. And then it came. And with it came a realization of what it would be like to see him angry.

He leant his hands on the table. His arms were very strong and muscular. "Now," he said, "I think you'd better listen to me for a minute." His voice reflected the force within him, and Eve sat very still, for tension crackled around them in that room like an invisible current, almost electric. "Nobody – *nobody* talks to me in the manner you're trying to do. That's the first thing you should remember. Secondly, I'm in charge here, not you, I will get us out of this place, and you back to Helsinki, and you will not suffer cold or hunger, I promise you that – but in return I expect common courtesy from you – something you have quite clearly never thought much about, for you're spoilt, selfish, completely without any kind of self-control at all –"

"I'm not going to listen –" she began, incensed.

"*Yes*, you are!" He banged his hand down hard on the table so that it rattled, and the vibrations shook her. "So shut up and *listen*. I've been very patient and forbearing. I've humoured your tantrums and your stupid childishness, but there's an end of it. Right now. We are here, and we are stuck here, miles away from civilization, and I personally don't care how long we stay for. I'll survive anywhere. And by God, I'm almost tempted to tell you to find your own way out, for if anyone needs a lesson teaching them, it's you, with your high-and-mighty, snooty manner. And the first lesson will be when you pluck that grouse – and we'll cook it together – and after that we'll go and catch a few fish from the lake – *together* – and you will do it, because if you don't if you start throwing one of your little tantrums, you'll damn well regret it. Do I make myself clear?"

She had to wait a moment before she could speak. Nobody had ever addressed her in such a manner before in her life. But Eve had an inner strength, and she needed all of it now as she tilted her chin defiantly and answered: "How will you make me regret it? Just

117

tell me that! You wouldn't let me starve – you just said that you wouldn't – nor would you throw me out of the hut – I know that too. So what will you do? Beat me?"

He gave a thin smile. "You've got guts, I'll say that. Perhaps you're not as soft as I thought. And you'll need them if you're going to stay here with me. Beat you? It's a tempting thought, but no, you're safe enough in that respect. Any man who could beat a woman isn't worthy of the name. But you'd find out soon enough, and I wouldn't advise you to try. I could tell you a few home truths about yourself that would make you cringe – and I would, believe me –"

"Words can't hurt me," she answered. "I wouldn't listen. You can't make me listen to anything you say, not if I don't want to."

"Is that so? But you do listen, don't you? You listen because you can't help it, because your vanity makes you. Look at you – just take a look at yourself in your mirror some time. You have a beautiful face, and you know it. I'm sure you've been told so often enough. And how long do you think you'll stay beautiful? True beauty comes from within, from the personality. Yours is such that in ten years you'll look hard and shrewish if you don't try and change what's inside you. The lines of discontent are there already – you may not be able to see them, but I can. In a while they'll be etched so deep you'll never get rid of them –"

"Shut up. Shut *up*!" Eve jumped to her feet and put her hands over her ears to stop the relentless words. And he came round the table and pulled her hands away, and held them.

"I told you you'd listen, didn't I?" His eyes gleamed darkly.

"You're hateful. You have no right –"

"Then I won't – if you behave yourself."

"Behave? You're talking as though I'm a schoolchild. What are you? A sadist or something?"

"No, not that. You'll see what I can be like if you co-operate. You'll find me very easy to get on with – and you can wipe that little disbelieving smirk off your face now because that's one of your expressions I don't care for. Why don't you try a smile occasionally? Can you smile?"

"Don't be stupid, of course – and you're hurting my hands."

"Then ask me nicely to let go. Try it. It'll not kill you."

"Please, Garth, let go of my hands," she said – and forced herself to smile. It was a bit trembly, but to her surprise he smiled back – and released her.

"There you are. Simple, isn't it?"

How she would have loved to hit him. How her fingers ached to strike that dark scarred face! But she dared not. It was beginning to sink in – very slowly – that here was a formidable opponent. Perhaps, just for a little while, she would humour him.

"I'll make the coffee," she said. "If I may." He ignored any slight sarcasm there might have been in the last three words, and nodded agreeably.

"Okay. And while you're doing that I'll clear the table ready for breakfast. Scrambled eggs do you?"

"That sounds fine. But – with powdered milk?" She tried to hide the horror she felt.

Garth laughed. "You'd never know – not the way I make 'em, I promise. Just leave it to me." It was true. There was an instant change in him. The unpleasant scene might never have been. He could switch effortlessly from sadism to something almost approaching charm.

They drank coffee and ate scrambled eggs from tin plates, with buttered crispbreads, and Eve was pleasantly full when she had finished. Then Garth produced a well folded, slightly tattered map, and spread it over the table, and, standing beside her, pointed to it. "Now, I reckon we're somewhere here," he said, and Eve tried hard to concentrate, but it didn't mean much to her. There was a vast expanse of lakes and forests and little else, as far as she could see.

"Oh," she said, "I'm afraid I'm not much wiser –"

"No. It's difficult, I know that." He leaned over, and his arm brushed hers for a second, and the touch was vaguely disturbing. It was a gentle touch, not hard, quite accidental. He didn't even notice, but Eve did, and wondered at it. "See, right up there, that's Rovaniemi – and way down here is Helsinki. You're with me?"

She nodded. "So far."

"Right. Now during that rainstorm, when everything went haywire, I was approximately there –" and his finger stabbed the map. "Allowing for time and everything just before the storm. So," he made a circle with his finger, "I reckon we're within this region –

and it's one of the most empty parts of Finland – and there are quite a lot of those." He laughed. "It's a country of wide open spaces, but I don't need to tell you that, do I?"

"No. So where do we go from here?"

"Well, later on I'm going to see if I can do anything to repair the engine. It's full daylight now. It was no good trying anything in the dark. I have a torch, but I won't use it unless necessary."

"And your radio? Is there a chance –" she tried not to sound too eager. But if he could get a message through, how simple it all would be.

"Don't raise your hopes too far, Eve. Of course I'll try, but –" he shrugged, "I just don't know. But we're going fishing anyway to the lake. We'll go soon."

"You've no fishing rods – or have you?" she added, seeing the growing smile on his face.

"Yes, I told you, I keep everything I need in the plane. It's like a home to me. There's even an inflatable dinghy. You won't know yourself, bobbing gently on the water, right in the middle, fishing rod in hand, while I paddle round looking for a place to anchor –" He frowned suddenly. "Eve? What's the matter?"

Eve, to her own complete horror and dismay, had felt tears pricking at the back of her eyes, and at his frown, his words – which sounded, strangely enough, almost solicitous, not cruel, she was no longer able to contain them. She put her hand to cover her eyes, just for a moment. "Nothing," she said, her voice muffled. "Really – I – I –" but her body shook and she felt his arm round her shoulders.

121

"What did I say?" he asked.

"No, no –" she shook her head violently. "It was nothing you said, truly. I just felt suddenly –" but she didn't know exactly what it was she did feel, so she stopped. How comforting was his arm. And how strange that it should be so.

"All right, Eve, just take it easy for a moment. Tell you what, sit down and I'll see if there's any coffee left to heat up."

"No, really – I – " she felt so incredibly foolish.

"No buts, I've told you, you'll have to learn to do as you're told," but his voice was gentle, not brutal, not at all unkind. "Sit down there and have a drink." And she did. "Okay. Better?"

"Yes." She swallowed the last drop. The coffee was strong with having stood for a while.

"Then we'll go. I'll roll up the oilskins and put them in my duffel bag, in case it starts to rain. There's no sense in us getting soaked."

She watched him work, precisely, without any wasted movement. Then he checked that the fire was safe, slung the rifle over his shoulder and pocketed the compass. "Ready, Eve?"

"Yes." She hadn't combed her hair or washed her face, quite unthinkable under normal circumstances, but here, in a way, it didn't seem to matter. She ran her fingers through the tousled tresses and jerked her head back. "I'm ready." she said.

He was right after all. Eve had never been fishing in her life; had never sat in a small boat in the centre of a tranquil stretch of water, with a fishing rod in her hand. But now she was, and it was having a certain effect on her. For it was like being in a different world. She could not have imagined it would be so; yet it was. A feeling of great calm and peace descended on her. There was silence, save for the occasional shush of water against the rubber dinghy. Distant bird calls were scarcely an interruption, merely part of the background. And Garth, who sat there with two wooden paddles, manoeuvring the dinghy occasionally, did not speak at all. The silence was not oppressive. It seemed that words were not necessary.

And then – a tug on the line, her excited squeal – his voice, calm and reassuring: "Don't jerk the line. Not yet, just pull, very gently, play it."

She followed the soothing words, obeyed the quiet voice, and when he said: "Right – now," she pulled in the rod, and saw the gleaming silver of a fish, felt it slap against her leg.

"Good girl!" His voice, warm with approval, was, strangely enough, exactly what she wanted to hear.

She caught two fish. Enough for supper and breakfast, he assured her. They left them on the beach when they went to the plane, and there she watched him fiddle expertly with dials and switches, and heard his disgusted: "Nothing. Dead as a dodo. God knows what's gone wrong. I'm sorry, Eve, it looks as though we're stuck here for another night at least. Come on, we'll get the fish back to the hut and decide what we'll eat, when." He helped her down from the plane.

Another selection of provisions from an endless-seeming supply being pushed down into his duffel bag first.

She was hungry again. She had never had such an appetite in her life before. It must be the air. She told him this as they neared the hut. It was easier to be civil, much easier. She still disliked him; would still take pleasure in telling him precisely what she thought of him, when the moment of parting came, but until then it was much simpler just to be agreeable.

"I know," he said. "It gets you that way. Probably it's the air. I eat like a horse when I'm staying in the wilds. It won't do you any harm. I mean, you'll not get fat or anything."

"How do you know?" she retorted.

"Because you're walking a lot, remember? Don't worry, you'll keep slim. Look at me," and he patted his flat stomach complacently.

Eve laughed. She couldn't help it. "You're a man," she said. "You're different."

"Really?" he seemed surprised. "Why?" They were nearly at the hut. He opened the door and they went in. It was like coming home.

"Well –" she lingered over the word, "you're active all over the place. Flying people, I mean. I can't explain it. But you must lead a very active life."

"Mmm, I suppose you're right. But you're slim yourself. You must keep on the move –" then he held up his hand. "Sorry, I'll rephrase that. You must keep busy." She knew why. He wanted to keep this fragile peace just as much as she did.

"Yes, I suppose so," she said slowly. "Please, I'm hungry. Is there any food?"

He laughed. "Okay. Tell you what – I'll put the fish on to cook now. One of them anyway, then, while it's cooking, we'll pluck the grouse ready for dinner. We'll dine in style tonight. Candles – wine – grouse with vegetables, followed by a sweet. How does that appeal?"

And all she could think of to say was: "Wine? Wine?"

He grinned. He looked very boyish when he did that. "That's what I said. Ask no questions. Just wait and see. All right?"

"Yes."

"Good. I'll do the fish. Will you tidy the hut?"

"Yes. Can I wash first?"

"Of course. I'll maybe shave later. I don't have an evening suit, but at least I can look civilized for dinner. Off you go and tidy yourself up, Eve. I'll fillet the fish and put coffee on."

The water in the barrel was icy cold and fresh. She felt better when she returned to the hut and found a hairbrush in her toilet bag. Garth was quite engrossed in his task at the table, a piece of newspaper ready to receive the bones, his fingers quick and decisive with the knife as the fish was filleted and put in a pan with butter – and something shaken out of a small jar.

He looked at her. "Herbs," he said. "Don't look so worried – I'm not about to poison you."

"I know," she answered. "I'm just watching." She brushed her hair vigorously. The feeling that had filled her at the lake was still with her. An ease, a gentle relaxed sensation; it was too much effort to worry. "That's better," he said, and put the pan on the glowing logs. "Your hair looks tidier now. It's good. I'm going to have a shave. You don't mind?"

"Why should I?"

He had a battery razor; as he watched the fish in the pan he ran it over his cheeks and chin. The faint buzzing reminded her of a bee humming as it looked into flowers. Stupid, of course, but that was the mood that possessed her. And it was nice. It *was* like home. She didn't care to analyse the mood, sufficient that it was pleasant. She sneaked a quick look in the mirror from her toilet bag. Her cheeks were a healthy pink, her eyes sparkled. And she laughed.

"Why are you laughing?" he asked, amused.

"I don't know. I've not put any make-up on today. I've never done that before."

"Hmm." He examined the razor, stroked his chin, put the razor in his duffel bag. "You look better without. Or is that rude?"

"Normally – yes. Today, I don't care."

"That's all right, then. We seem to be getting on well. Had you noticed?"

"Yes."

"Good. Shall I show you how to prepare the grouse? We can stick it in foil and let it cook all by itself while we get on with other things."

"All right, anything you say." Then she put her hand to her head. "What am I saying? I've just realized. Nobody knows where we are, do they? No one at all. My father thinks I'm at Heli's – and Aunt Sofia, will she be worrying? Do you think she'll be concerned – and Esko and Liisa?" She looked at him wide-eyed, suddenly remembering.

He shook his head gently. "Search parties, you mean?"

"I suppose so."

"What do you want me to say? That they'll be sending out planes? I'm sorry, Eve – but no, they won't. Aunt Sofia will just imagine you've forgotten. Esko and Liisa aren't expecting you. Your father – well, you know better than I. But it seems to me that there's no one who'll be at all concerned, not for a few days anyway. I'm sorry, Eve."

He looked it too. He came over to her and touched her shoulder gently. "Don't worry, we'll get out safely, I promise you that. Now, shall we do the grouse?"

She closed her eyes. His touch was reassuring in an odd way. "Yes," she said, and mentally prepared herself.

They spent the hours after lunch chopping wood. At least Garth chopped the wood, Eve watched, and stacked it neatly. "It is essential," he told her, as the axe cleaved the logs, "to leave the wilderness huts as you find them. Someone – the previous tenants – had left a solid stack. We must do the same." She admired the precision of his movements as he swung the axe blade through the air. There was a strength about him, a calmness that had already reassured her.

"I know," she said. "You told me before."

127

The perspiration beaded his brow. The rain had gone, the sun was high and, although not strong, was warm. Eve had put a jacket on; Garth had removed his. Shirt-sleeves rolled up to elbows, he was an impressive figure of a man standing there. And Eve, sitting there, was content just to watch him.

"It's the code of the wilderness," he said. "It works."

"I'm sure it does." She sat back on her log. She knew she should be worrying about something, but she couldn't think what it was. Daddy wouldn't really be missing her; not yet. So what was it?

"It's like a rule. You accept. Do you know what I mean?"

"I think so. Did I make a good job of the grouse?" She surprised herself with the question. What on earth did it matter?

"You did. You learn quickly, Eve." She felt a glow of pride at his words. Absurd, of course – what did *his* opinions matter?

"Ready for your next meal? One you've practically cooked yourself?"

"Nearly. But I'm not working at the moment, am I?"

"You want to have a go at chopping wood?" He looked faintly astonished.

"I wouldn't mind."

"Have you ever done it before?"

"No, but as you said, there's always a first time."

"Fair enough. It's not woman's work, though."

"That could have the Women's Libbers down on your neck," she retorted.

He laughed. "You scare me! I mean, there's a knack

128

in it, and forgive me, but you don't look very strong."

That did it. Eve stood up. "You've said quite enough," she answered. "That is practically a challenge. Just stand clear, that's all."

He handed the axe to her. "It's all yours." And he was grinning again. Not with mockery, though. Just waiting. He thought she would make a mess of it. Eve, with a new-born confidence in her ability – especially after watching him at work – knew she wouldn't.

The axe swung through the air and went cleanly into the tree trunk, on which the logs rested, missing the wood by several inches. "Damn!" she exclaimed, and glared defiantly into his laughing face.

"The tree trunk is only for standing the logs on," he said patiently. "You're not supposed to chop *that*."

"I know, I know. Just wait. I'll do it now. You see." And she did. She chopped the waiting wood neatly in two, then in two again. What a quiet satisfaction there was in throwing the cleanly cut pieces on to the growing pile and picking up the next branch. After a few minutes she had to take her jacket off, and threw it to Garth to hold as he sat patiently waiting.

"I – told – you – I'd – do – it," she said between chops.

"I was sure you would," he answered.

"Were you? You didn't *sound* sure," she paused to flick back hair from her eyes.

"Because it put you on your mettle, that's why," he explained patiently. "And stop when you've had enough. You're using muscles you don't normally use. You'll ache all over tomorrow if you do too much."

She wanted to retort that she didn't care, that they would be away from there anyway, but it would be tempting fate to say anything like that, and in any case, the vaguely disturbing thought returned suddenly, and she knew what it had been that had worried her before. He had said, in response to her query about planes and searchers: "Not for a few days anyway." He had said it with a certain sureness that had sent a quick shiver of apprehension up her spine as she heard it. Yet he also kept telling her that they would soon be away – as if it might only be a few more hours – and then those hours passed, and then several more. Was that why they were already searching for their own food? Because he *knew*? Because it could be days and days? She stopped chopping. This was as good a time as any to have it out once and for all. To *know*.

"Garth," she said, "can we get one thing straight now?"

He frowned, very slightly, more a narrowing of his eyes – as if he anticipated her question. "You sound very solemn," he said. "What is it?"

"Just give me an honest answer to an honest question," she went on. "How long exactly do you think we'll be here?"

"You want it straight? Okay, I'll tell you. Another three or four days." It was not such a shock as she feared. Because she had already mentally braced herself for such an answer.

"But – why – why did you keep pretending that – that –?" she paused, because the words she wanted, quite strangely, would not come. She felt weak.

"That it wouldn't be long?" he asked almost gently. "Because I didn't think you could take too much at once, that's why. But now you've asked, and I owe you the truth, I can tell you. You'd better sit down, Eve."

"No, I'll stand." What was there in his voice, on his face? What could be worse than what she already guessed and anticipated?

"I'd rather you did. Please," he said, and patted the log beside him. "Come on, you've been working hard. And what I've got to say is difficult to explain."

Eve walked over towards him, dropping the axe. A shiver of apprehension touched her face making her cold, despite her bodily warmth. "What is it?" she whispered.

"You know I told you we're lost? And you know I went out very early – alone – this morning? It was because I suspected something, and now I'm pretty sure I'm right. Eve, we must be very careful before we set off walking, or trying to find our way out of here –"

"I don't understand –" her voice was quiet. She was breathless. It was an effort to speak.

"I know. It's not easy for me to explain. But it's a combination of several things. The least of our worries is that we're practically in Russia – and we don't have visas –" it was said in a lightly joking tone, as if to lessen the blow of what was to come. "But the thing that worries me is the animal population hereabouts. There are not only bears, but I think I saw a wolf lurking in the trees – and where there's one of those there will be more. They're a pack animal. Don't go far from the hut, Eve, whatever you do."

131

CHAPTER NINE

THE words were mercifully slow in sinking in. And when they had, Eve swallowed. "Oh, I see," she said quietly.

"So," he went on, carefully and slowly, "we're not going to rush off madly, are we? We're going to reconnoitre first, and plan our moves carefully. And tonight, when it's dark, I'm going out alone to try and get our bearings. I can do it if I take the map and torch – and if I find a few more lakes –."

"No," she said. "Not alone. I'm coming with you –"

"It's too risky," he cut in. "I'm used to scouting in the dark. I can move silently –"

"I don't care!" She turned to him. Eyes wide, she felt the colour in her cheeks because of her exertions, knew that she must look a sight, but it was no longer important. "I'll learn how to move silently. You can teach me now – in daylight. I'll help you, carry the torch and compass. But you don't leave me alone. Not there, not at night."

"And how well do you climb trees?" he asked.

"Trees? I don't see –"

"I mean, could you shin up a tree fast if we saw a bear or a wolf? Or would you panic and start screaming?"

Was it some nightmare, or was she really here? She took a good deep breath. "Try me," she said. "Show me how to climb a tree – and then watch me do it."

He laughed. "I don't believe it! You think you can learn in five minutes? Oh, come on –"

She jumped to her feet. A wild recklessness filled her. Before she could think about what she was doing, she grabbed his hand and began to pull him to his feet. Unresisting, he allowed her to do so, a half smile beginning on his face, lifting his wide mouth, crinkling his eyes.

"In *those* trousers?" In a minute he would be laughing, she knew that. But it wasn't anger which filled Eve. There was no room for temper with the sensation that filled her. She felt as if she was coming *alive*. It was the oddest feeling. Her eyes sparkled.

"I can buy more," she retorted. "What's a pair of trousers?"

He shrugged. "May I have my hand back, please?" And she realived that she was still holding it. "Your eloquence persuaded me. Okay, wood-chopping session over for a while. We'll carry the logs back to the hut and then have climbing lesson number one. Are you *sure*?"

"Oh, quite sure," she answered. "*Quite* sure!" and she began to laugh. His glance on her was amused.

"Can I share it?" he asked. "The joke, I mean?"

"If anyone had told me, only a few weeks ago, that I'd be stuck here, in this absolutely remote place, chopping wood, de-feathering dead birds – and learning how to climb trees, I'd have steered them fast to the nearest psychiatrist. But now here I am. And perhaps," she sobered slightly, "if I wasn't laughing,

133

I'd be crying. So now you know." And she nodded.

"Mmm, well, I'll tell you something now, Eve. You're a girl of constant surprises, do you know *that*?"

"Am I? In what way?"

He was bending now, busily piling the cut logs into their precious cardboard box, which was already showing signs of wear and tear. He looked up at her. "It's all right, you can take that light of battle from your eyes. I mean it as a compliment. You adapt yourself remarkably well to the suddenly changed circumstances of your life. That's good." How could she have ever imagined she would appreciate compliments from *him*? But somehow his words held more meaning for her than any of the fulsome praises she was accustomed to hearing from others.

"I don't have much choice, do I?" she pointed out, darting forward to pick up several logs which tumbled from the loaded box as he stood up. She piled them in her arms and began walking back towards the hut, leaving him to follow.

"True," he admitted, as he caught up with her. "But a person's attitude can make a heck of a lot of difference. You were playing hell with me at first – remember? Or should I now shut up?"

"It might be better," she rejoined sweetly. "Seeing that we seem to be getting on reasonably well – for once."

"And I still have to teach you how to climb trees. Hmm," he nodded. "And I don't want my teeth kicked in as I help you up. Point taken."

"I shouldn't think you're very frightened of me,"

134

she answered. "You seem to be quite accomplished in the defensive arts, if I remember rightly."

They were at the hut now. She pushed the door open and held it for him to pass her with his loaded box. "Judo? Ah yes. Do you want to –"

"Learn it?" She laughed. "Not today, perhaps. There's a limit to what one person can do in a day –" she stopped, sniffed deeply. "There's the most exquisite aroma –"

"The grouse!" Garth put the box down in a corner and went to the fireplace, prodding the silver foil wrapped parcel with expert care. "Hmm, nearly done. And it's –" he looked at his watch – "too early for dinner yet. Never mind, we'll do the trees first. That should give you an appetite – if you haven't already got one, that is."

She sighed. "I have," she confessed. "What are we eating with it? And what's for afters?"

"Is that all you ever think about? Food?" he asked severely.

"Here, yes."

"You'll have to be patient, then, won't you?"

"Then I'd better wait outside. The smell of that bird is making me positively faint."

He came over to her and took her arm. "Don't think about it. Mind over matter. Come on, Eve. Oh, have you any gloves?"

"I think so."

"If they're not madly expensive I'd put them on if I were you, or you'll ruin your hands."

They were in her handbag – exquisite black leather,

to match the bag. She took them out and put them on. Garth gave a low whistle.

"I can –" she began.

"I know. Buy more. Don't say it. I'd better knock them off my bill. I can see you returning to England with a sadly depleted wardrobe. However –" he shrugged and held the door open.

Returning to England – those three words, so casually spoken, had an odd effect on Eve. For that was precisely what she would be doing, quite soon, just as soon as possible in fact. She should have felt her heart lift at the words. But she didn't. She didn't know why. There were beginning to be a lot of things that she didn't understand about herself.

The tree was frankly terrifying. Not to look at, because it was rather beautiful – but viewed as something to climb – and Eve started at it aghast.

"Watch me, Eve," Garth's voice was quite matter-of-fact. Clearly it held no horrors for him. "Because I'm going up a little way, just to show you – then you can try."

They were near the hut. Half hidden by intervening trees, she could see the smoke curling up from the small chimney. "All right," she answered.

He didn't make a great show of it; he simply climbed up, shinning upwards like an agile boy, using feet and hands, grabbing branches – and then stopping when he was well over her head and grinning down at her.

"You see?" he called. "Dead easy when you know how."

"I forgot to tell you – I can't stand heights," but her attempt at a joke was lost as he swung his way down and leapt nimbly to the ground.

"Come on, I'll start you off, although it's cheating. Come here, let me give you a leg up." She walked cautiously nearer to him, as if he might pounce on her and bundle her up it. She couldn't back out now. She *couldn't*. But she wished she had had the courage to say no.

And then it was too late. Foot in his clasped hands, a lift – and she was clinging for dear life to a very sturdy-looking branch, scrabbling with her free foot for a huge knot in the bark. And then – quite suddenly – it was easy. Because from there she saw an even better branch, and one for her other foot, and she was free of him, clinging, then climbing, pausing, seeking hand-and foot-holds, going upwards with an ease that took her by surprise.

She stopped and looked down, saw him begin to clap politely at her performance, and she started to laugh.

"I like it!" she cried. "Why haven't I tried this before?"

"You should have been a boy. All right, you can climb. Come on down now, Eve."

She should have known it was too easy. Going down was more difficult. But she managed it, moving carefully, feeling her way until, as she was almost at ground level, he reached out to hold her. Just for a moment his arms were round her. He, laughing, Eve not quite laughing – because his touch was disturbing. She twisted free, and smiled. "Phew! Did I do all right?"

"You'll pass. No bear would catch you. Okay, tree climber, lesson's over for today. Dinner will be served in ten minutes. And seeing how well you've done, why don't you go and freshen up, skip round the hut – keep out of the way for a few minutes? I'll shout you when you can come in."

She stared at him, puwled, and he grinned. "A surprise, okay? Just do as I ask."

"As you wish." She winced as she touched her hair. "One request first. Can I have my handbag?"

"Of course. I'll fetch it."

The door opened, then closed, then opened again. "Catch," he said, and threw it to her. "And don't come in until I call you."

Some imp of mischief prompted her reply, a memory of his words. "Yes – *boss*," she answered. And grinned at him.

The door closed very firmly, and she pulled out her tongue. Then she sat down on a large boulder and began to do something with her tousled curls.

The door opened slowly. "Okay, Eve, come in."

"Are you sure?"

"I'm sure. Dinner, as they say in the best circles, is served."

She rose from her seat on the boulder and walked gracefully towards the door. Hair brushed and shining, gloves in bag, a touch – a mere touch – of lipstick on her mouth. Eve was ready – and very, very hungry.

She stopped inside the door. Just stood still and looked at the table. For a second her eyes deceived her.

Just for a brief moment it seemed as if she might be entering a quiet little French restaurant. Two candles gleamed and flickered slowly on the table. Plates were set, and cutlery – and napkins. She stared. "Napkins?" she said in utter disbelief.

"Paper hankies, actually. Part of my secret store. But you're not supposed to look too closely. Please sit down, madame." He pulled out the bench for her, and Eve sat down. Nothing would really have surprised her. In the gleam of the candles, even the metal plates looked as though they were made of heavy silver.

Garth served the grouse, and with it small peas and carrots. What if they were obviously from a tin? Nothing else mattered save the fact that the fowl was succulent and mouth-melting. Eve tucked in with great enthusiasm, relieved that Garth was doing the same, or she would have felt guilty. What was the matter with her? She had never had such an appetite.

"Oh, Garth, that was superb," she sighed, as she pushed her empty plate away.

"I'm so glad Madame is pleased. And now the sweet." She had forgotten that. "The Seton Special. Alas, the ice cream didn't arrive – but perhaps you'll enjoy it on its own." And he produced the "Seton Special" with a flourish.

He had mentioned "afters", but she had forgotten about them. It was quite a simple dish, tinned fruit and chocolate sauce – but with it he poured out a beaker of white wine for Eve and himself.

"One only, I'm afraid," he grinned. "If we're going

out looking afterwards, we'll need our wits about us. You're enjoying it?"

"Mmm, yes. You're wasted in your job. You should have a restaurant somewhere."

"You reckon so?" He sipped his wine thoughtfully. "It's an idea. Like the wine? I bought it in Rovaniemi. There'll be enough for tomorrow."

She sniffed her wine in its metal cup. "Ah yes, a brave little fellow – possibly '68, would you say?"

He matched her mood instantly. A moment's thoughtful pause, a gentle licking of the lips, as if pondering, then: "I would have said '70, actually – that *was* an excellent vintage. We can ask the wine waiter when he arrives with the liqueurs if you like."

"Ooh, will you?" Eve's eyes sparkled. "And I only drink Napoleon brandy with my coffee – black with just a little sugar."

"The brandy?" He looked faintly alarmed.

"The coffee, idiot!"

"Sorry. Of course – Napoleon. What else?"

There was a fragile magic around them. They were perfectly in harmony. It was like – what is it like? thought Eve, looking at him. There's no friction, no tension now. We're both perfectly relaxed, at least I know I am, and it must be the same for him. It was growing darker, so that the warm yellow candlelight caught his face, softened it, made him look devastatingly attractive. What on earth's the matter with me? she thought. I'm sitting here with a man I don't like, having just enjoyed what should have been a very ordinary, even primitive meal, but there's something in the air, something I can almost reach out and touch, and I can look at him now, and see him more clearly than I ever have before. And he's not the aggressive peasant type I thought him to be at first. He's different from anyone I've ever met before in my life.

"Penny for them?" his amused voice brought her back from her reverie.

She shook her head. "Sorry. I was lost in admiration for your cooking." At least it wasn't a lie.

He stood up. "I'd better get coffee, before a painfully swelled head gets in the way."

"Let me get it, please."

"No." He held up his hand. "This is *my* meal. You'll get your turn tomorrow. I mean, you can do an entire dinner if you want."

Eve looked at him. What did she say now? I'll try, but I don't think I'll be much good? Somehow she didn't want to admit her ignorance.

"I'll do my best." She swallowed hard.

"You will? Good. I shall look forward to that."

It was no use. She would have a sleepless night worrying about it if she didn't confess right *now*. "But I'm not – I'm not as good as you, I don't think. But I will try."

"That's all I need to hear. Look how well you did when you tried to chop wood – tried to climb a tree. You succeeded, right?"

"Yes, but it's not quite the same –"

"Yes, it is. You'll see."

He went to make the coffee, and had to go outside for

141

water, and Eve was left alone to think briefly over his words. There was an imperceptible sense of change within her. She had never regarded it as an important asset before, the ability to cook. There had always been someone else to make meals, someone else to see that fires were made, that life ran smoothly and comfortably. They were not subjects on which she had ever pondered. There had always been more important and interesting things to think about. And now, quite suddenly, those other, more interesting things had palled. and the inevitable question intruded. How would John or Neil have coped here? She knew the answer.

Garth made it all seem easy. — although it could not be. And, more important, he made it seem fun. That was the big difference. He had said something about having the right attitude. How well he practised what he preached! His air of balanced calm was soothing and constantly reassuring to Eve.

She watched him now as he returned, went to the fireplace, crouched down on his haunches to watch the water boil, ready to fling in coffee at the right moment. She stood up, and going over, crouched beside him.

"I just want to say," she said quietly, "that I don't think I've ever met a man so infinitely capable and resourceful as you."

He grinned suddenly. "Thank you." Then, as if he didn't really want compliments: "Do you really want your coffee black?"

She laughed. "Only if there's brandy with it."

"I said there was, didn't I?"

"You're joking! I mean – *I* was only joking," she amended hastily.

"I wasn't. There is brandy. Not, alas, Napoleon, but a creditable alternative. It's something I always carry with me. Strictly for medicinal purposes, I might add. No booze when flying, that's my motto."

Eve stood up slowly. "I can't believe it! You'll be telling me next that you carry a full scale medical kit."

He looked up at her. "And that too."

She went slowly back to the table. "You'll be telling me that you're a doctor as well in a minute."

"Not quite." Then, seeing her face, he laughed. "Was that a wild stab in the dark, or a joke?"

"Why? *Are* you?"

"I was going to be, but after five years at university I decided it wasn't for me. So now you know. If you sprain your ankle – or anything else – I'd make a fair job of looking after you."

"Oh!" she gave a deep sigh. Suddenly she saw, as if in a scene unfolding, the complete emptiness, the barren waste, of her own life. She had done nothing, never worked, always led a gay butterfly existence. And this tough-looking man could do almost anything he wanted. The depths to him were almost incomprehensible.

"Any more surprises?" she asked, with an attempt at lightness, prepared for anything.

"Mmm." He was thinking. "I have a degree in philosophy. But that's nothing." He shrugged. "And I studied psychology as well." He frowned. "Do you really want me to go on?"

143

"Yes." She really did want to know. "There's *more*?"

"You're making me feel awfully conceited. It can't be good for me, you know."

"Never mind. Tell me." Then she added: "Please, Garth."

"All right, don't say I didn't warn you." He poured out the coffee and fetched a flask of brandy from his duffel bag, then sat down. "No, never mind. It's stupid –"

"Please. I'm interested – honestly."

"Here goes then. Degree in philosophy – economics – M.A., B.Sc. – and oh yes, I rowed for Cambridge. We won. And I boxed for the University and ran in the Commonwealth Games –"

"I don't believe it!" But she did. "No, of course I do. You're incredible!"

"Well –" he drawled the word, and hung his head. "Gosh, ma'am, Ah'm sure blushin' now –"

"And of course you've lived in America. That accent!"

"For a couple of years, yes. I worked my way from ranch to ranch, I've always been interested in horses. In fact, one day I think I'll have a racing stables. When I've got tired of flying. And you, Eve. What have you done? More important, what do *you* aim for in life?"

"I'm beginning to realize I've done nothing. As for an aim in life," she looked at him, and it hurt, "I don't know. I wish I did." There was a lost empty sound to the words that she could not avoid.

"You must have some idea. Write a book? Marry a millionaire?"

She laughed. At last it was near enough to a laugh. "Something like that." The coffee was waiting. She sipped it and thought about things. She did not, she definitely did not want to talk about herself. She looked at the brandy. And Garth, seeing her glance, perhaps knowing, said: "Ah yes, brandy." He unscrewed the flask and poured a measure into the lid, then an equal amount for himself in a metal cup.

"Cheers," he said.

"Cheers." She sipped. It was a surprisingly mellow cognac. She didn't know what she had expected. He lit a cheroot.

"We'll go out soon. Wrap up warmly. Put on your extra sweater."

"Do you think – we'll get our bearings? And – be safe?" she asked.

"I hope so. We'll take the map, torch and compass – and the rifle."

"And when – if – we get them. What then?"

"Then we'll know the right direction to walk in, won't we?"

She sighed. "Yes."

"Why the big sigh?" He seemed only mildly curious.

"I don't know."

"A good enough answer. You women are illogical creatures at the best of times."

"Oh, are we?" She found that quite funny. At one time it would have made her furious, now his remark didn't seem important. "Why?"

"Because." He shrugged. "Just because you *are*, that's why."

"And that's a completely illogical remark for a start," she responded. "Coming from an expert in psychology – and philosophy."

"*Touché*!" He swallowed his coffee, then sipped the brandy, looking at her across the table. "I forgot to tell you, I took a course in logic too. So your comment struck home even more forcefully. Still, perhaps it's just that I don't want to start an argument. After all, we're getting on quite well at the moment, aren't we? and it's quite logical not to want to spoil that."

Eve smiled at him, quite unconscious of the fact that if the candlelight was doing things for him it must be doing things for her as well. So that she didn't understand the darkening of his eyes, the sudden way his mouth closed, the reason he looked away, just for a moment. Then it passed, everything seemed normal again, and he stood up.

"Shall we go?" he said. His tone was fractionally cooler.

"Yes. I'll get a sweater on." She didn't know what was the matter, but her heart beat faster.

He stoked up the fire, collected the things they needed, moved methodically, as he always did, and when they went out of the door, everything was normal again. Outside he touched her arm lightly. "This way," he said. "Towards the lake. We'll study that – see if we can actually plot its shape, then find it on my chart. And then –" he paused, "we'll take it from there. Okay, Eve?"

"You're the boss," she answered, well aware of what she was saying.

He laughed, amused. "Will you repeat that into my portable tape recorder some time?"

"Don't tell me you have one of those too?"

"A battery one, yes. We could sing duets on it – if you need a good laugh, that is."

"But I might have a superb voice," she retorted lightly.

"Ah, but *I* haven't, I promise you that. I could always do a Lee Marvin-Telly Savalas type take-off, you know, speaking the song, but apart from that –" he shuddered.

They were moving towards the lake – their lake. And the atmosphere was just right again. It was a clear cold night, with a good sized moon to make the torch unnecessary. "It's quite a relief to know that you're not perfect at everything," she answered. "I was beginning to feel so useless before –"

"I don't believe that."

"It's true. But I can sing, I really can."

"Go on, let's hear you."

"*Now?*" she stifled laughter.

"Why not? The night is young, we've got quite a bit of walking to do – no one to hear you except me, a few assorted birds, the odd bear – or two –"

"All right, I take your point. But give me time. Later, perhaps."

He shrugged. "Okay. Now, we're nearly there –" then he stopped, took her arm and said, very softly: "Shush – listen."

CHAPTER TEN

SHE froze. A prickle of fear ran up her spine as they both stood perfectly still. And then she heard it – a faint crackling sound from the undergrowth nearby – a shuffling, slithering – Eve clutched Garth's arm in terror. She was trembling. He pushed her, gently, silently, against a tree, and his voice was the merest whisper in her ear: "Stay still."

Then he was unslinging the rifle. She heard the click as he pulled the catch. Then the wait. She stood perfectly motionless, because he had told her to do so, and whatever he was feeling, it wasn't fear or panic. He was as calm as always, but keyed for action, ready for anything. And with that sudden realization, all her own fear melted away. She knew in that moment that she should never be frightened with him.

An explosion of sound, but in miniature, the scuffling intensified – then a scampering noise, dying away. Silence. And in the silence, Garth began to laugh, softly at first, then more loudly.

"What was –?" she began, still a little tremulous, the sensation of relief almost as weakening as her previous fear had been.

"Who knows? A couple of hares fighting, would you believe? I haven't a clue – but it wasn't a bear or a wolf, thank God. Are you okay, Eve?"

148

She took a deep breath. "I am now," she answered. "Thanks to you."

"Me? What did I do?"

They were continuing towards the lake. "You were so calm – so unafraid. I felt utterly *safe*," she whispered.

"Why are you whispering? It's nice to know I can inspire confidence anyway. I must confess I wasn't at all sure myself."

"Oh yes, you were! I can't imagine you ever being afraid of anything."

"I like it, I like it! You do realize, don't you, that my ego is getting highly inflated? Is this the 'be nice to Garth' evening? Because if so, don't let me stop you –"

"I've said enough," she went on. "So I'll shut up." But the good atmosphere was still there; it was *right*. She could not have explained why, not even to herself. It was as though she was beginning to see the real Garth for the first time. The image, the memory of how she had first seen him, was blurring and slipping out of focus. And Eve knew that it was because she herself was changing too. She didn't know in what way – but she knew it was good. She felt more alive, more alert than she had for ages. It was all because of him, of the way he behaved. To think that she would actually enjoy a primitive meal in an even more primitive hut – yet she had. And now, to be wandering through the night, trying to find a bearing, with a man she had thought rude and aggressive – who among her friends would believe that she was actually finding the experience stimulating and agreeable? Not one. They would think she was mad.

"But I'm *not* mad," she thought, and then, horrified, realized that she must have said it aloud, as Garth, in a very amused voice, told her:

"I didn't say you were!"

"Oh! No, I didn't mean – I was thinking, I'm sorry. I didn't know I'd –"

"Never mind apologising. I'm fascinated. What brought on the vehement denial?"

It was useless to try and lie. He was practically a mind reader anyway. "I was just thinking about my friends, and how dotty they'd imagine I was if they knew what I was doing – and that I was actually enjoying it," she explained.

"And are you? Enjoying it, I mean?"

They were at the lake now, near the plane, and the moon shone down on the black calm waters, illuminating everything with its ghostly sheen, casting the stark outlines of the surrounding forests into even blacker shadow, so that the entire scene was like some stunningly beautiful painting, black, white – dramatic.

"Yes," she said quietly, "I am."

"That's good," he said casually. "Let's sit down for a moment here, shall we? No, there, on that flat rock. It'll be quite dry. Then I can get my torch out and we can have a look at the map."

Eve obeyed, waiting for him to sit beside her. If I don't *think* too much, she thought, if I just *accept*, it'll be easier. Because there was a turmoil inside her that

150

she couldn't explain, nor did she want to try. And she wondered then why she should tingle at the very nearness of the man who now sat beside her, big, casual, unflurried, unfolding the map, flicking on his torch. Garth Seton. A man she had really thought she could never like, not in a million years. And now – and now – she wanted very much for him to kiss her.

"I'm sorry?" Confused, she turned, because he had just said something, only she hadn't heard the words above the idiotic pounding of her heart.

"I said that I'm going to walk along the lake as far as I can. Do you want to come with me or stay here?"

"Come with you," she answered promptly.

"You're feeling quite energetic?"

Oh, if only he *knew*! "Quite energetic, thank you."

"Okay then, off we go." He flicked off the torch, stood up, and held out his hand to help her up. Surely, she thought, he can feel how I tremble? But apparently not. He set off at a brisk walk, with Eve beside him. On and on along the side of the lake, now slowing where the ground was uneven, now more quickly when there were no rocks or pebbles to impede their progress, and all the time curving round, following the lake's own natural contour. Somewhere, distantly, a bird gave a shrill call, which was answered. Then silence again.

I could walk for ever, thought Eve, for ever and ever . . .

One second it was clear moonlight, or so it seemed; the next, they were completely surrounded by swirling mist. Or had they walked into it? Eve couldn't be sure, so engrossed had she been in watching the back of Garth's head as he walked in front of her.

"Damn it!" he exclaimed, and turned towards her. He was laughing. "This is all we need."

"What's happened?" They had been about to enter the trees again, having seen enough of the lake to know, from the map, which one it was. He had already marked it with a pen. And now they were going to go back to the hut to decide the best way – the safe way – to leave.

It wasn't like fog at all, but it was thick and damp and clinging. Eve breathed in, and it was like being underwater. She reached out to touch his arm, not frightened, hardly nervous, but seeking that trace of reassurance she needed.

"Mist from the lake – don't worry, we'll be away from it in a minute – I hope. I should have seen the warning signs. Take my arm, I'll guide you through the trees." But then he put his arm round her shoulders, so casually, and that seemed better than anything else. Crackling twigs and leaves underfoot made a ghostly accompaniment as they went inwards, in among the trees. And the mist swirled and whirled round them. She could feel it in her hair, on her eyelashes and brows. And it had gone very cold. She shivered. "Brrh!"

"We'll soon be home," he said. "You see." And he squeezed her arm at the top, near the shoulder, where his hand rested.

Home! That was what he had said. How odd to call a wilderness hut home! And yet – and yet in a way that was what it would be like. To open the door, to go in to where a welcoming fire waited. Yes, it would be like coming home.

"And when we get there, I'll make us coffee," said Eve. She was beginning to feel tired now. They had been away for over two hours. And it could take them another one to get back, so Garth had said, just before the mist swirled in from the water.

"If you're still awake," he answered, teasing. "You sound half asleep."

She yawned. "I'm not," she denied. Then: "Well, perhaps a little bit tired. But only because it's late." And then she stumbled, because you could scarcely see your feet at all, but Garth gripped her hand so that she did not fall.

"Thanks," she said.

"Be careful," he answered. "Shall I walk in front to guide you?"

"*No* – no," the first one had come out too vehemently. She didn't want him to think she liked him holding her. "I'll watch what I'm doing."

"Poor little Eve, poor little girl," he said softly.

She looked up at him. "Why do you say that?" She was more curious than annoyed.

"Because that's what you are. You should be safely tucked up in your sleeping bag fast asleep, not wandering through forests and mists with me."

"Oh dear, don't start that again." She managed to stifle that yawn. "You know, you can sound incredibly patronising at times. You should know by now that women are as strong as men in lots of ways –"

"Yes, yes, I know. Please don't give me a lecture now. We're getting on so well. I know! Let me hear you sing. That will keep us both awake, won't it?"

She looked up at him. "But –"

"No buts. You *said*. You told me you were good. So I want you to prove it. Now tell me, what can you do best? Pop? A touch of opera?"

Suddenly her mind went blank. She couldn't think of one single tune.

Garth cocked his head. "Mmm? Lost your tongue?"

"I can't remember –" she began feebly, well aware that it would sound like a pretence.

"All right, let me. Let me see – what about a good oldie to begin with? Do you know any of the Beatles? 'Hey Jude' – 'Yesterday' –"

"Oh, I've thought of one – 'Country Roads'. Can I sing that?"

"Can you? The stage is all yours, my dear." And then, dropping instantly into a mock American accent that sounded remarkably like a mixture of all the disc jockeys on all the pop shows: "Let's have a sincere welcome for little Evie Carrick, who I guarantee will bring a tear to your eyes with her rendition of 'Country Roads'. Take it away, Evie baby!"

"You idiot!" she burst out, overcome by sudden and helpless laughter. "You expect me to sing after *that*?"

"Of course. You would if you were on 'Top of the Pops'. No point in being self-conscious about it. Just let it all rip."

What did it matter anyway? She had never been self-conscious in her life. She wasn't going to start now.

Although – although *this* man was having a strange effect on her. Eve began to sing, softly at first, then with gathering confidence because she knew she had a good voice, and instinct told her that she sounded well. She finished the song and then looked at him.

"Hey, you know something? You can sing. That was super." He wasn't being sarcastic. He meant it. A warm glow filled Eve. How strange that a few words from Garth could please her so much.

"Thank you, kind sir. Now let's hear you do your bit."

"But I told you I can't –"

"You made me sing. Fair's fair. Do that one of Telly Savalas' – you know, that big hit he had a while ago. 'If a picture paints a thousand words' – you *know* it. Everyone knows it. I'll help you if you get stuck."

"Don't say you've not been warned –"

"Coward!"

"All right." He shrugged. "But you can sing it with me, like those girls do in the background, or else –"

"Right, I will."

And they did. They had just finished it as they reached the hut, mist-swathed, cold, ghostly-looking, and the memory of one line haunted Eve as they went inside, shivering with relief. "If the world should stop its turning, spinning slowly down to die, I'd spend the end with you –"

I would spend the end with you. She turned the words slowly over in her mind as she watched Garth cross to the dying fire, saw him kneel to put some more logs on, and she kept her eyes on him with a kind of hungry intensity of which she hoped he was unaware, because she could not have looked away from him even if she had tried. If – she thought – if the world should end, right now, I'd be with you, and I wouldn't be frightened of anything, because – because – and at that second he looked round, looked directly at her, his eyes meeting hers in the shadowy flickers from the now blazing fire. He stood up slowly and came over to her.

"What is it, Eve?" he held out his hands and took hers. "Oh, but you're freezing. Come and sit by the fire." She allowed him to lead her to the warmth. She felt as though she was in a dream. Everything had become misty, unreal, almost as unreal as outside the hut.

"There, sit down. I'll make the coffee. You can supervise."

"Yes." She clasped her hands in front of the bright yellow flames.

Gradually warmth seeped into her. I didn't think it would hit me like this, she thought. I never imagined that the knowledge would come with such force, or affect me in such a way. She felt incredibly tired. And she wanted to reach out and touch him, and say: "I know that I love you, Garth – and isn't that strange, because I loathed you at first." But she didn't.

She accepted the coffee, and when he poured in a capful of brandy, she made no demur. I love him, she thought, in a kind of growing wonder, that was filling her being. I love him – and he's scarcely aware of me at all. And in a few minutes we'll both get into the same sleeping bag – and it will all be terribly impersonal, because to him I'm a passenger, an encumbrance, someone he has to look after –

"Okay, Eve?"

"Mmm? Yes, fine, thanks. Have you found out where we are?" She could be impersonal as well – when it was necessary.

"I think so."

"Good." She put her hand to her head. "Do you mind if I get ready for bed?"

"For heaven's sake! It's past one. Of course! Tell you what – you go outside and wash your face, I'll tidy up in here. Don't get lost now."

"I won't." She managed a smile.

When she returned, he had tidied the table of cups, and spread the map out. "Get into bed. I'll not be a moment." But he looked at her as he spoke, and she wondered if something showed in her face. She smiled.

"All right. Do you need help?"

"No," he shook his head. "Just a few calculations. How's the mist?"

"The same." She yawned. "You don't mind?"

"Off you go. Fish for breakfast. Remember?"

"Mmm. And it's my turn to cook a meal. I've not forgotten that either." She scrambled into the sleeping bag; never had any bed seemed as comfortable. She lay on her back, watching the dancing shadows on the dark ceiling of the hut. If she turned her head she would see Garth sitting at the table. She would in a minute. She was savouring the moment, knowing she was here, *now*, with him, and that was all that mattered. I've changed, she thought in wonder. I've changed com-

157

pletely in the space of a few days, and it's all because of him. He has opened my eyes, made me see what life can be all about. And it's all happened by accident, by the misfortune that made us get lost in a storm.

Then she knew that she had found the contentment for which she had been searching for so many vain months. She closed her eyes for a moment. Too soon it would be over. He doesn't love me, she thought, without bitterness. Why should he? I have behaved like the little spoilt baggage I was – was, but am not now. Life will be different when I get back home to England. There will be a time to evaluate my life – and my friends. I shall start to do something useful with my time in future. First a visit to Heli – for she would understand, she above anyone, a true friend – a rarity, Eve knew that now. And in a way, Heli was responsible for her meeting Garth. Oh, the talks we'll have, she thought.

She could hear the faint scratching of pen on paper, and she turned her head slightly to look at him at last. You'll probably never know, she thought, but I thank you for letting me see everything in a true light, instead of the distorted mirror through which I viewed life before. And then, because she was exhausted, she closed her eyes. And slept.

She awoke early the following morning. The contentment of the previous night was still with her. She had slept deeply and well, and felt full of energy. Beside her, still deep in sleep, Garth lay on his back, one arm half covering his face. Eve smiled softly, gently to herself. It was his turn for a surprise. Breakfast in bed. If only she could wriggle out of the sleeping bag without disturbing him. She didn't know how late he had stayed up the previous night, for she had been fast asleep from the moment of closing her eyes.

She had managed it! Creeping across the hut for her shoes, Eve carried them outside before putting them on. The mist had cleared slightly, and it promised to be a hot day, for already her face felt warm in the pale sunlight that was managing to filter through.

She built up the fire twig by twig until it crackled into flame and she was able to put larger branches on. She knew now how to wrap the fish in foil, how to put it in where it would have maximum heat. And when that was cooking she began to boil water for coffee. And still he slept.

She combed her hair, after changing her sweater and trousers, felt her face still tingling from the icy cold washing water, and debated whether to bother with make-up, then decided against it. She hadn't even looked in a mirror for what seemed like ages. She smiled to herself.

The water boiled, and she brewed coffee, and poured out two beakers full. Then she went to rouse him.

"Garth. Garth, wake up." Gently touching his arm, wondering if he knew how her hand trembled as she did so.

"Hmm?" A sleepy blinking, a yawn, then he was stretching, nearly awake. "Eve? Is it morning? Good grief!" He sat up and ran his fingers through his hair.

"Good morning. Coffee is served. And breakfast

won't be a moment." She handed him his beaker. "There you are – sir."

"This is too much," he murmured. "What have I done to deserve it?"

"Nothing. I just thought it was your turn to be waited on."

"Hmm, don't let me stop you. Beautiful coffee." He sipped appreciatively.

"Thank you, but I don't really have time to talk. If you'll excuse me I'll get on with my work," and she bobbed him a curtsey and went to set out the plates and cutlery.

She had begun the day well, and that was how it continued. He told her after they had eaten that he still wasn't sure enough of where they were to risk setting off walking. Absurdly, her heart lifted at the news. "You mean we must keep looking?" she asked him. "Fine. Just let me know when you want to set off. I'm ready. And shouldn't we chop more wood today?" This with a glance at the diminishing pile of logs.

"You don't mind?" He had seemed surprised.

"No."

"Good. I was dreading telling you."

She had nearly told him then *why* she didn't mind. It was on the tip of her tongue. But she didn't, of course. She had gone to busy herself with tidying up while he checked the map preparatory to setting out. She wanted to sing. Her mind was full of songs now, and after a while, when he was outside, she began to hum happily.

Late evening, and she had never felt so tired – nor so happy – in all her life. They had spent a busy day chopping wood, fishing, walking for miles without seeing a single wolf or bear – and the sun had been high and hot, and she knew, even before he told her, that freckles were appearing on her nose and cheeks. She carefully avoided them normally, by using sufficient make-up, and keeping out of the hot sun, but now it didn't matter.

He peered across the table at her as they ate a welcome supper of baked beans and crispbreads – something she would once have regarded with horror, but now enjoyed – and he said: "You know you're covered in freckles?"

"Yes," she nodded quite happily. "So what?" this flippantly.

He grinned. "So nothing. I thought you'd like to know, that's all."

"I imagined I would be. That sun was hot today." She pushed away her plate and stretched. "Oh, that was good! What's for breakfast in the morning?"

"My God, woman, is that all you think of?" he frowned at her, but she knew he was finding it difficult not to grin.

"Yes." And she smiled, then said: "Oh! Ouch!"

"What is it?"

"I've just realized, my shoulders are aching like mad. I was too hungry to bother before, but now we've eaten the pain's come back."

"That's all the fancy axe-swinging you were doing. I told you to stop when you got tired, didn't I?"

"Yes, oh, master," she said meekly.

"Hmm, and not so much of the cheek either, or I won't rub your back for you," he retorted.

"Oh, would you?" She hid a giggle. There was a thought! Would she be able to bear it, though? He would be quite impersonal, she knew that, but the effect on her could be quite different. There was only one way to find out.

"Have you some liniment?" she asked.

"I have. Stay there and I'll get the first-aid box from the plane. I'll not be five minutes. You can clear away the supper things if you like, while I'm gone."

"I'll come with you –" she began.

"No need. I'll run both ways." He was already getting up as he spoke.

"So long." And he was gone, closing the door after him. As she stood up to move the plates, Eve looked over towards the door – and saw the rifle. He had forgotten it! She went cold. He never went out without it. Quickly she opened the door, and shouted his name, and the trees caught it and sent back mocking echoes. But there was no answering shout. Nothing. If he saw a bear – or any wolves. Suppose – suppose there was one – suppose – Eve closed her eyes, her vivid imagination supplying the images she didn't need. Then without further thought, she picked up the rifle and rushed out into the night after him.

Of course she would meet him on his way back. He had said he would run, and she imagined he would be unbeatable at that. But she didn't. And she reached the lake, apprehension clouding her mind. Could she have missed him? And then she saw it – a light from the plane. Her breath came out in a sigh of relief as she walked quickly, quietly towards the water – then she stopped, because she heard a voice, Garth's voice – and she knew what was slightly odd about that light from the plane. It wasn't torchlight – it was the interior lamp. She was about to shout his name, with a mixture of delight and puzzlement, when she heard what he was saying, and she stopped in her tracks and stood quite still, because something was wrong, oh, so very wrong.

"Yes, the 'treatment' has been effective, tell him, so tomorrow, by some miracle, I'm going to get the plane working –" then he laughed. To Eve, standing there unable to move, the laughter had a harsh ring to it. "– that's right. Oh sure, she's a different girl – chopping wood, climbing trees – you'd never believe –"

She had heard enough. Blinding waves of realization flooded her. He was talking about *her*, about Eve herself – and talking on the *radio* – which was working perfectly, as was the interior light, which was supposed to be dead. She didn't completely understand it, but she was filled with a sickening sense of horror, and the desire to get away from there.

She dropped the rifle – and then heard Garth's voice: "Eve? My God, Eve –" Then she turned and ran. She didn't know where she was running to, only that she wanted to get away. Blinded by tears, choked with racking sobs, she heard splashes, then running footsteps. On and on, into the forest she went, but the tears so filled her eyes that she could only see dark blurs for trees, and in her chest was a terrible pain from running – and the pain of betrayal – and everything was coming in on her, shadows falling, a distant man's voice telling her to stop – to stop . . .

She didn't see the tree. She couldn't see anything now. She ran smack into it, and the cruel branches and twigs scratched and struck her, but the pain was not as great as that knowledge she carried. The world exploded in a colourful whirl of stars and agony, and Eve fell back, mercifully unconscious.

CHAPTER ELEVEN

But eventually Eve had to wake, and when she did she was on the sleeping bag in the wilderness hut, and Garth was bending over her.

"Eve," he said gently, "don't move. You're hurt. I'm going to dress your wounds –"

"I don't want you to touch me –" It was an effort to speak, in more ways than one. Her face felt swollen, and she could scarcely move her mouth. She felt warm salt tears on her lips – or was it blood? Did it matter? She wanted to die.

"I must. You'll get infected if I don't. Sip this first. It's brandy." She felt the cool metal at her lips, his hand behind her shoulders lifting her very gently.

She sipped, and the spirit stung her mouth, but it went down, and warmed her, gave her strength.

"I want to sit up," she managed to say.

"I wouldn't advise –" he began.

"I want to *sit up, damn* you –" and she began to struggle upwards.

"All right." He assisted her, and now she could look at him properly. She was trembling. He sat on the edge of the platform, and watched her.

"Do – do you want to know something?" she managed to say. "I – I – thought I was g-getting really like you – and now I *hate* you. Do you hear me? I *hate* you. W-what have you got to say to that?" She could not help the treacherous tears now. They coursed down her face, burning and stinging her skin where it had been scratched. "Because I know that for some reason of your own you've deceived me. Are you laughing? You should be. You did a great job. You made me believe the plane wasn't working. That was a lie, wasn't it? There was nothing wrong with it – answer me, please."

"Yes, it was a lie. There's nothing wrong with the plane, never has been."

"Then why – why?"

"Have a drop more brandy." She took the small beaker from him, and then, with unerring accuracy, flung the contents into his face.

He didn't move, or speak. Nor did he attempt to wipe the spirit from his face. "I hope that stung you," she said. "Then you'll know what mine feels like."

"Eve, I'll tell you everything – when I've done something with all those cuts and scratches –"

"I told you, you don't touch me –!" Her voice shook with intensity.

"I will if I have to hold you down while I do so. And I'm a damn sight stronger than you, so I advise you not to fight me. Then we'll talk."

Her ribs hurt horribly and she put her hand on her side. Pain was making her dizzy now, but she would not, would *not* give in.

"You'd better take your sweater off as well. Show me where it hurts."

"I won't – I –" She stopped, gasping for breath.

"Lie down." It was easier to yield than to resist. She

166

lay back, and now she began to wonder if she was going to die after all.

"Can I take your sweater off?"

She couldn't answer. She opened her mouth to try, but no sound came out. Then she managed: "I'm frightened –"

"I know. Don't be. You're safe with me, I promise you. But I must look at your ribs. Trust me now, Eve, just trust me." His voice was so infinitely comforting. If only she had not heard what she had! If only . . . Then the pain became simply too much. She saw his face become blurred, and then it faded away into a roaring blackness . . .

Strange how comfortable she was now. All pain was gone, and she opened her eyes to see Garth sitting there quite still beside her, quite still. He must have seen the flicker in her eyes. "It's all right, Eve, I've given you an injection to ease the pain. And I've bandaged your ribs. I'm quite sure you've not broken any, but you've got a helluva bruise there."

She put up her hand to touch her face. "Don't," he said. "I've cleaned the cuts, they'll all be healed in a day or so, I promise you that. But it's better if you don't touch your face for a while."

"And are you going to tell me why – *why* –" she faltered.

"If you're ready to hear it. Yes."

"Oh, I'm ready all right. And then I want to leave here."

"You won't be going anywhere for a couple of

days, Eve. You need rest. Your body's had a heck of a beating –"

"I'm not staying. Not with you"

"Listen to me. I'll tell you now why we're here. I owe you that, after what you heard – oh, God, if only I'd remembered the rifle –"

"You mean you were enjoying the pantomime? Yes, I see –"

"You don't. You don't at all. I'll begin at the beginning, which was a few days ago, when you were at Esko and Liisa's. That was when the idea first came to me, but I thought it was too preposterous for words, and put it out of my mind, like some pipe dream – until, when we were at Aunt Sofia's and I brought you coffee – remember?"

"Yes." She didn't know what he was talking about.

The words weren't making sense. She could hear them all right, but there was no meaning to them, none at all. And Garth as if he understood touched her hand. "Do you want a coffee?" he asked. "The water's boiled. It'll not take a minute."

"Yes." She was beginning to feel drowsy now. Perhaps the coffee would wake her. She wasn't sure if she wanted to stay awake, to hear what he had to say, because already there was a growing sense of bewilderment within her – and hurt. Not only physical, but mental; an awful aching hurt because she was remembering some of his words over the radio, and knew now with icy certainty that they were a message to be passed to someone about her. "Oh, sure, she's a different girl."

"Sit up, Eve. I'll help you – that's it. Now sip it slowly. I've put sugar in because it's good for shock." She wouldn't have had the strength to fling this in his face if she had wanted to. She sipped it, and it was good and strong, just what she needed.

He went on, because it was as if he sensed she was ready for his story: "In your bedroom at Aunt Sofia's, I decided, quite simply, what I was going to do with you. I was going to let you have a taste of the simple life you so despised – partly to teach you a lesson, and partly –" he hesitated, the merest shadow of a smile touching his mouth, "because I thought it was what you needed. And so I went about it, quite cold-bloodedly. I knew where I was going to bring you, and I knew *how*. All I had to do was wait for you to want to return to Helsinki. And then get us 'lost.'"

"And that's what you did." Her voice was blurred, because the sharp edges of pain were dulling her senses. And yet the overwhelming mental hurt was there, and she felt tears coursing down her cheeks, stinging the cuts, and her whole body began to tremble. Garth touched her.

"Don't cry," he said. "Please don't cry. You're strong, Eve, stronger than you believe."

"I don't feel strong." She kept her voice steady with an effort. She didn't hate his arms being round her, strangely enough. Because her own hatred was draining away and her body felt deliciously light as if she might float away. . . .

His voice had been fading, and then it stopped. Eve stirred slightly, felt herself being gently laid down, and her last thought, before she drifted off into sleep, was: I hope he doesn't move away.

She woke to pain, and a stabbing, blinding headache, and cried out involuntarily.

"All right, Eve, I'm here." It was nearly light, and she saw dimly that the table was beside the sleeping platform, and that Garth, now sitting up, had been lying on it. "I'm here," he repeated. "I'm going to give you a couple of pain-killers."

She took the pills from him, and the cup of cold water, and swallowed them. "What time is it?"

"Nearly eight. You slept soundly."

"And you – you slept on the table?"

"Yes. I was warm. I had a couple of blankets in the plane. I went to get them after you fell asleep."

"Can I sit up, please?"

"If you want to. I'll help you."

When she was sitting, he pressed a hand to her forehead. "Have you got a bad headache?"

"Yes. How did you know?"

He gave a wry grin. "Because I think you have a touch of concussion. Hardly surprising, the way you dashed into that tree. And I really think you'd be better lying flat."

"After I've been outside."

"I'm coming with you."

"No, you're not. I can walk."

"You can't – look, I'll just come out –"

"No." She looked at him. "I'll manage by myself."

"I think you will." He unzipped the bag, and helped

170

her to stand. For one terrifying moment she thought her legs would not support her, and then, taking a deep breath, and with his arm around her, she made her way to the door.

He opened it. "Are you sure you –"

"Yes!" It became easier after the first few steps, even though the world swayed alarmingly around her. But Eve's determination carried her along. "I will not fall," she said to herself. "I *will* walk. I will."

But when she reached the door of the hut again she had no strength to open it. "Garth," she said – and he was there, before her, almost before the word was out of her mouth.

He took her arm, guided her over to the sleeping bag. There was a smell of coffee. "Are you hungry?" he said.

"No. Tired. But I want to hear –"

"Yes, you will. Lie down. Carefully, gently does it."

She was better lying down. The headache was fading to a distant throb, her ribs only hurt if she took a deep breath, so she avoided doing so.

"All right. I'd been in contact with Esko and Liisa before I arrived and although they didn't say much I had this mental image of a selfish, spoilt little bitch –"

"And you weren't disappointed when you met me," she interrupted, with a poor attempt at a smile. Behind the smile, the tears were well hidden.

He sighed. "No – I wasn't, Eve. In fact I was quite looking forward to taming you –" He stopped, ran his fingers through his hair. "I didn't realize how difficult this would be. If it's any consolation to you, I feel an utter swine for being responsible for you running into that tree."

"It helps a little," she said wryly. "Please go on." The anger, the sheer hurt, the horror of it all, were fading slightly. She could almost listen to him impersonally, as if he were talking about some third person, not there. Perhaps that would be the best way after all.

"I telephoned Esko – as you so shrewdly guessed – on Monday morning, to tell them what I planned. They were horrified, as you can imagine – but I told them that officially they knew nothing – that if your father phoned, as far as they knew you were still in Rovaniemi, whooping it up at Aunt Sofia's. But I promised to let them know how I progressed. Esko's a radio ham, and getting in contact with him from the plane was no problem. That was when you overheard. Otherwise you'd not have known a thing, would you?"

"No," she answered quietly. "I'd not have known a thing. What if Heli had been at home?"

He shrugged. "Nothing. I'd have had to wait a little longer, that's all. I also phoned for a weather report that morning. I had it planned roughly where I intended to bring you. But if the weather had been too good it would have been a problem doing my dramatic landing. I flew deliberately into that rain. But there was no danger to us at any time."

She was weary of it all. "I'd like to sleep now, if you don't mind," she said quietly.

"Of course." He stood up. "In a couple of days we'll

be ready to go. I shall come back to England with you. You're not fit to travel alone."

She didn't answer. She closed her eyes. Oh no, you won't, she thought. Oh, no, you *won't*. But she didn't say it because she didn't want argument. She lay there, listening to the sounds he made as he moved around the hut. There was no anger at all left within her. But she had thought she loved him; at least that ridiculous notion had gone for good. All that was left in its place was a curious kind of blankness, a numb feeling. At least she could now see people – her friends in particular – more clearly. That at least Garth had done for her. John and Neil had receded so far into the background that she knew they would never occupy any space in her thoughts again. The thoughts became hazy, too difficult to think clearly. Imperceptibly, Eve slipped into a restful sleep.

He left her several times during the course of the day. To chop more wood, to check the plane, to fetch water, and each time he told her how long he would be, and she accepted this, and lay resting until his return.

And when it was night again, he gave her another pain-killing injection that gentled her into sleep within minutes.

She felt so much better the following morning when she awoke that she actually wondered if she was still dreaming. Then, very slowly, she sat up. Instantly he was awake.

"Eve? What is it?"

"Nothing. I'm sorry I woke you. I'm feeling much better. I was just seeing if it was real."

"Good. You have marvellous powers of recovery. But take it slowly at first. Are you hungry?"

"Yes." Much to her surprise, she was.

"Then I'll make breakfast. Would you believe – fish?"

"Anything will do, thank you."

It was easy now. Quite easy to be polite. Because he was like a stranger. She had no feeling left for anything – or anyone. And especially not him. She wondered how she would feel when she reached home and met her friends. That was yet to come. But for Garth, she felt absolutely nothing. It made everything so simple.

If he saw, he made no sign. He was gentle, and efficient, and caring. Once, just once, when she had been in the middle of eating her lunch, she had looked up suddenly – and had surprised a strange look on his face. Just for an instant, but it would have puzzled her – if she had been sufficiently interested to care. It was a deep, dark expression, like nothing she had ever seen before. She had looked down to her food again, uncaring. But she was to remember it, much later.

Saturday morning came, and she was well enough to travel, he had decided. So had Eve. All that had been in her mind since the previous day was the sheer determination to be fit and able to escape. For that would be what it was in a way for her. Escape from him, that was what she craved. Freedom to lick her wounds in private, and recover. Not so much from the physical injuries but the humiliation of the whole situation. To be used as a sort of guinea-pig – that was something she would never forget as long as she lived. But she would neither forgive nor forget the man who had changed her life. She watched Garth as he tidied the hut preparatory to them leaving. He worked quickly and efficiently. He was carrying everything to the plane and then returning for Eve.

I wish I could leave before you return, she thought, but I know that's impossible. There's nowhere to go and you would soon find me, but just as soon as I can I will escape, and then you will not see me again – ever. And so she bided her time, because she knew that it would not be long.

He went, loaded up with luggage, leaving only his sleeping bag and duffel bag. "I won't be long," he told her.

"I'll wait for you," she answered. She looked round the near-empty hut, stripped of all the personal possessions that had made it seem almost like home. Home! she echoed the word. What a hollow sound there was to it now. And to think that she had once trembled at his touch, had begun to feel stirrings of a new, heady emotion. That was all over.

She looked into the ashes of the dead fire, and shivered. Then she knew that there was one question that neither of them had considered, and it must be asked. As he came back into the hut, she asked it.

"I forget," she said. "Did it work?"

He looked blankly at her. "I'm sorry. What do you mean?"

Eve stood up. "The experiment. The plot. *Me*. Has it worked?"

"Ah." He nodded. "What do you think?"

It wasn't the answer she had expected. It wasn't any sort of answer at all.

"I'm asking you," she said quietly.

"You've changed. Yes," he answered. "You're a different girl from the one who arrived. But whether it worked or not, that's something that only you can answer – in time. But to see you now – and to remember you as you were at Esko and Liisa's – there's a great deal of difference."

"Yes, I know." She nodded slowly. "You must be very pleased with yourself." She looked round, unwilling to meet his eyes, which were disconcertingly clear and bright. "We'd better go."

"Yes, I suppose we had." He slung the duffel bag over his shoulder and picked up the sleeping bag. "Take my arm, Eve."

"I'll walk on my own, thank you." She smiled at him. "Really, I'd prefer it. You can catch me if I fall."

"As you wish." He shrugged. Then he was shutting the door behind them. Eve did not look back. It seemed miles to the lake, and once or twice she faltered, but she would not let him help her. "I can manage, thank you," was all she said. How could she tell him that it was practice for when she left him at Helsinki? For he thought he was returning to England with her. Eve knew better. Her strength was gradually coming back to her. She would find a hotel in Helsinki to stay the night, and then fly home the day after. How she would leave him she had not yet considered. Her passport, ticket and money were all in the handbag she carried. He could hardly take that from her. She had already packed nightdress and toothbrush in her small make-up case. He would just have to send the rest of her luggage on, her name and address were clear enough. But she didn't really care anyway. Oh, for a hot bath! That was all she needed. And perhaps a good meal, served in her room – and time to think, and consider what had happened. She lifted her chin, and walked straight and tall towards the plane. And she didn't see Garth watching her.

"And I suppose the nearness to Russia, and the hairy stories of bears and wolves were all figments of your imagination," she said.

"No. They were real enough – but neither bears nor wolves would have attacked us without provocation," he answered.

"So it was just another part of the ploy to keep me from wandering off – or trying to," she answered. "You know, you should be writing plays or books – you'd make a fortune."

"Would I? Perhaps I'll give it a try some time." He made sure she was comfortable. The sleeping bag was wrapped round her, and she leaned back on a blanket. He made coffee for them too, in the flask, and she only had to ask.

"What will we do when we reach Helsinki?" she said very casually.

"Leave the plane, get a taxi to the airport, and then home. You feel up to it?"

"Oh yes, of course." But she smiled to herself. He was in for a shock. Serve him right when she vanished. She wondered what he would do, but she didn't really care. Leaning back, she closed her eyes. She would rest now and save her strength for later. What bliss it would be to be alone, with time to think. Perhaps she would stay there for two nights and go home on the Monday . . .

"Wake up Eve. We're here." His voice was an intrusion into a disturbing dream, and she woke instantly. They were still, only the slight movement of the boat on water now, and no engine sound. How far away the wilderness hut seemed now! Like another world – and that of course was what it had been. And now, she thought, I'm going to adjust to being my own normal world again – only things will never be quite the same. With a calm dignity, she allowed him to help her from the plane, and on to dry land.

She looked around her. They were clearly on the outskirts of the city, for the lake was surrounded by trees, and nearby there was a scattering of houses, but no traffic noises.

When he had brought her cases and his bag, she sat on one while he locked the plane door. Sat and watched him, happy in the knowledge that soon she would be away from him. Perhaps at the airport, she didn't know, but it wouldn't be long now. She was vaguely hungry, but that could wait.

"Now, I'm going to get us a taxi," he said. "You'll stay here? Will you be all right?"

"Of course. Don't be too long."

She watched him go, saw him running across the grass with long athletic strides. No one passed, save a dog that came up, sniffed curiously at the cases, then wandered off again with a slight wag of its tail. Eve lifted her face to the sun. What a bizarre situation it was! Unreal, yet at the same time, almost as if part of an inevitable pattern.

She heard a distant sound, a car, and knew it was Garth returning. She had her handbag and make-up case. The rest he could manage. Whatever happened, she would not be parted from those.

They were soon at Helsinki airport, and he put the luggage in the main hall, thronged with people, and said: "I'm going to see about a plane for us."

"Wait," Eve said. "I must go to the Ladies first. I look a sight."

"You don't —"

"Please," she said. "I'll not be two minutes."

He looked at his watch. "Of course. I'll stay here."

She didn't say goodbye. She didn't want to. She smiled and walked away slowly. It was all very clear in her mind now. There were enough people about to make it easy. She went into the door marked "*Naisille*," and there was another exit, well round the corner. It was too easy for words. Far easier than she had anticipated. Head down, just in case, mingling with the tourists, walking, and out into the sunshine to where a taxi was cruising along. Eve raised her arm. The next minute she was inside, thumbing furiously for her guide in Finnish, to tell the man to take her to a hotel – any hotel.

CHAPTER TWELVE

THE room was warm, too warm, so she opened the window and looked out, down to a busy street. In a minute they would be bringing lunch up, and she waited quite patiently. She had her own little bathroom and shower, and her skin tingled with cleanliness. After she had eaten she would telephone her father, then she would have a rest.

And that was the afternoon taken care of, but what about the evening? There was a bar, and a television room, she had seen those on the way up, and she might go down and watch later, because there would be plenty of time to think when night fell, and she was truly alone.

The discreet knock at the door, and she went to open it. A waiter stood there with a small trolley, and covered dishes.

"Do you speak English?" she asked.

He smiled. He was middle-aged, round-faced, pleasant. "A little."

"I wish to make a phone call to England after I have eaten," she said, speaking carefully.

"Yes, yes, very simple. You have your own telephone – just pick up and ask the reception. All speak good English. They will get your number for you."

"Thank you."

He pulled up her table, laid it with gleaming cutlery,

lifted the lids off steaming dishes. "I will serve you, miss?" he enquired.

"No, thank you. I'll manage."

"Please ring if you need anything."

"I will. Thank you."

Alone again, she tucked into smoked salmon, tender lamb, vegetables. Bliss! She had been more hungry than she realized. She wondered what Garth was doing. Perhaps waiting patiently outside the Ladies' loo at the airport? Somehow, she thought, I doubt it. He would have asked the attendant to search it by now, and then what? He would know, of course, but he wouldn't know *where* she had gone. He might try Esko and Liisa's, but that would do him no good, because she wasn't going to get in touch with them. There was no point.

She finished eating and picked up the telephone.

She told her father on the telephone call about the visit to Aunt Sofia – and about Heli being away – and then she told him that she and Garth had got lost. His concern crackled over the wire, nearly exploding the receiver. But when she told him of the wood chopping, the fishing – the tree climbing, she sensed a change in him.

"You enjoyed *that*?" Incredulity vibrated over the ether.

"Funnily enough, yes. Then I had a slight argument with a tree – but that's another story –" it was quite easy to keep her tone light.

"But you'll be all right to travel home? You're sure?"

"Fine. Really fine. Just as long as you meet me. Promise?"

"Tell me where you're staying and I'll call you tomorrow to check what time you'll be at London Airport."

She told him. She had to pick up a packet of book matches to spell the name out, and she said good-bye and hung up. It was nearly four o'clock. There was time for a rest, then a light meal, television, a drink or two, and bed. Eve lay down on the bed and fell fast asleep.

When she had made up carefully, the scratches were almost invisible. The cut on her lip was the only problem, but even that wasn't too noticeable. She brushed her sweater and trousers carefully, picked up her bag, and went downstairs.

The service was pleasant and unhurried, and she drank wine with her light meal, then made her way to the lounge to watch television. It didn't matter that she understood nothing. There were magazines – English and American – to read, and waiters to bring in drinks, and the evening passed pleasantly. She wasn't tired when she decided to go up to bed. But it was nearly eleven, and she was going to get everything sorted out in her mind once and for all. Tomorrow she would go for a few long walks, and on Monday her father would see the new Eve. She said good night to the friendly waiter and took the lift up to her room.

The light gleamed softly under the door. She had left

the bedside lamp on, as she always did in hotel rooms, so that the place would be more welcoming. She turned the key in the lock, pushed the door open, and went in. Garth stood up from his seat by the window, and came towards her.

"Hello, Eve," he said. "I've been waiting for ages."

Shock held her rigid by the door. For a moment she went dizzy. "It's all right," he said. "Sit down. I thought this might be a surprise." He pointed to her table on which stood two glasses and a bottle. "Perhaps you'd better have a drink."

"Please go away," she said weakly.

"No. Not again." He took her arm. "Come and sit down. We've got things to talk about. I've brought your cases, incidentally." She saw them outside her bathroom door.

"But I haven't told Esko and Liisa where I am," she began. It was easier to sit down, so she did so, on the bed.

"You didn't need to. I got your father's number from them and phoned him because I imagined you would contact him."

"W-what did you tell him?"

"Not the truth. Not over the phone. But I intend to later – I owe him that. I merely said you'd forgotten some of your luggage – which is true, in a way. Then I registered here, told the receptionist I'd brought on your cases, and said I'd wait for you."

"Why?" she asked.

He filled her glass and handed it to her. "Brandy," he said. "It's good for shock, remember? Drink up.

Why? I've told you, we have things to talk about. I don't like leaving things unfinished."

"There's nothing unfinished," she answered slowly. "It all finished the minute we left the wilderness hut – or perhaps before, when I heard you talking over the radio." She looked up at him. "The game is over, surely? What more is there?"

"A lot." He sat beside her on the bed. "I don't feel inclined to let you out of my sight now. Not after letting you injure yourself. I shan't forget that."

Eve twirled the glass before sipping. "Then I absolve you from all responsibility," she said lightly. "I'll even give it to you in writing if it'll make you feel any better."

"Eve, look at me." The glass was taken out of her hand, then Garth was turning her face towards him, his hand gentle under her chin. "I don't know how you're going to take this, but I realized, just two days ago, that I'd fallen in love with you."

She began to laugh, softly at first, then helplessly, until her laughter was stilled by his mouth on hers. Just like that, no subtlety, he stopped her, his arms going round her in a way that brooked no resistance. And after the first few moments she didn't try.

Endless magic, the kiss, like nothing before, and when it was over, he looked at her, his eyes dark and gentle. "Now laugh," he said.

Her mouth trembled. "I don't want to," she whispered. "Oh, Garth –"

"Oh, Garth," he mocked. "Is that all you can say? Where's the fire?"

"I came back here to think," she said, "and now I can't. Why didn't you just leave me be? This is no good. I'm the little spoilt bitch, remember?"

"Perhaps once, perhaps, ages ago. Not now. You're not the only one who's changed. It's happened to me too. I didn't ask to love you, I didn't want it to happen, but it has, and if it takes me forever, I'm going to make you love me –"

"I don't think it will take that long," she said softly. "In fact –" and then she stopped.

"Yes?"

She shook her head. "Never mind. May I have my glass? I think I need that drink now."

He passed it to her. "You can't stop in mid-sentence. In fact – what?"

"It came to me one day, in the hut, that I loved you. But then – when I found out the truth – I went so numb, I thought I'd never feel anything again." She cradled the drink, fighting back tears.

"Oh, Eve, oh, my dearest love, don't cry, please don't cry. I've been a brute. I must have been mad to have ever thought up that scheme. But I did. Now I've got to live with it. Nothing you can say will make me feel any worse than I do, believe me. But to see you weep just tears me in two."

"Then you'd better go, because I can't help it. Please go, Garth. Leave me on my own." She looked at him. "Please. Now."

Her mind was a turmoil of conflicting emotions. "We can talk tomorrow. I'm not going to run away. again, I promise you."

186

He stood up. She remembered that strange expression that had been on his face in the hut, for in an odd way it was there again. And now she knew what it was. He turned away and went towards the door. Then, just before he opened it, he turned to her. "Good night, Eve," he said. His eyes were dark with pain, his mouth straight, the skin pale around it. But he held himself straight and tall, and in that instant she knew she couldn't just let him walk out, not like that.

She stood up slowly. "Wait." Crossing the room towards him, she put out her arms in an instinctive gesture. No words were needed. His arms went round her, and they just stood there, all tension, all unhappiness melting away in a few silent seconds of perfect wordless communication that were in a way timeless. She could feel the beat of his heart against her. Then he touched her hair.

"Hello, my sweet Eve," he said. She looked up.

"Hello, my dear Garth." The smile on his face was like nothing she had ever seen before. It was beautiful. She knew it was reflected in her own.

"Do you think," he asked thoughtfully, after quite a long while, "that we'd enjoy a honeymoon in our wilderness hut?"

Laughter bubbled up inside Eve. "Where else?" she answered.

Amanda Doyle

A Change For Clancy (#1085)
Clancy hadn't liked the new trustee-appointed manager of Bunda Down, Jed Seaforth—but when Johnny Raustmann threatened him she somehow found herself emotionally involved.

Play The Tune Softly (#1116)
Ginny's joy in her new job at Noosa was shattered when she found Jas Lawrence there—the one man she never wanted to see again.

A Mist In Glen Torran (#1308)
There'd been many changes at Glen Torran, but Verona was dismayed to find Ewan MacKinnon still expected to inherit her along with his brother's estates.

Iris Danbury

Rendezvous In Lisbon (#1178)
Janice Bowen went into the impossible Mr. Whitney's office to resign. Instead, she found herself agreeing to accompany him on a business trip to Lisbon!

Doctor At Villa Ronda (#1257)
Nicola usually ignored her sister Lisa's wild suggestions, but this time accepted her invitation. She arrived in Spain to find that Lisa had mysteriously disappeared.

Hotel Belvedere (#1331)
Andrea took on a job at the luxury hotel where her aunt was head housekeeper, only to find her life becoming increasingly and dangerously complicated.

A GREAT IDEA!

We have chosen some of the works of Harlequin's world-famous authors and reprinted them in the 3 in 1 Omnibus. Three great romances — COMPLETE AND UNABRIDGED — by the same author — in one deluxe paperback volume.

Joyce Dingwell (2)

The Timber Man (#917)
It was bad enough to have to leave Big Timbers, but even worse that Blaze Barlow should think Mim was leaving for the wrong reasons.

Project Sweetheart (#964)
Alice liked being treated as though she were something special—she privately believed she was. Then Bark Walsh, the project boss, suddenly ended her reign!

Greenfingers Farm (#999)
It never occurred to Susan that circumstances were not as they seemed, and that her well-intentioned efforts as companion, were producing the wrong results!

Mary Burchell (2)

Take Me With You (#956)
Lucy fought hard for a home of her own—but it was her return to the old orphanage that provided the means to achieve it.

The Heart Cannot Forget (#1003)
Andrea didn't take Aunt Harriet seriously about inheriting her estate until she met her aunt's dispossessed and furious nephew Giles and his even angrier fiancee.

Choose Which You Will (#1029)
As companion to old Mrs. Mayhew, Harriet expected a quiet country life—but quickly found her own happiness at stake in a dramatic family crisis.

LOOK WHAT
YOU MAY BE MISSING

Listed below are the 26 Great Omnibus currently available
through **HARLEQUIN READER SERVICE**

Harlequin Reader Service

ORDER FORM

MAIL
COUPON
TO ➤

Harlequin Reader Service,
M.P.O. Box 707,
Niagara Falls, New York 14302.

Canadian **SEND**
Residents **TO:** ➤

Harlequin Reader Service,
Stratford, Ont. N5A 6W4

Harlequin 🔷 Omnibus

Please check Volumes requested:

- ☐ Essie Summers 1
- ☐ Jean S. MacLeod
- ☐ Eleanor Farnes
- ☐ Susan Barrie
- ☐ Violet Winspear 1
- ☐ Isobel Chace
- ☐ Joyce Dingwell 1
- ☐ Jane Arbor
- ☐ Anne Weale

- ☐ Essie Summers 2
- ☐ Catherine Airlie
- ☐ Mary Burchell 1
- ☐ Sara Seale
- ☐ Violet Winspear 2
- ☐ Rosalind Brett
- ☐ Kathryn Blair
- ☐ Iris Danbury
- ☐ Mary Burchell 2

- ☐ Amanda Doyle
- ☐ Rose Burghley
- ☐ Elizabeth Hoy
- ☐ Roumelia Lane
- ☐ Margaret Malcolm
- ☐ Joyce Dingwell 2
- ☐ Anne Durham
- ☐ Marjorie Norell

Please send me by return mail the books which I have checked.
I am enclosing $1.95 for each book ordered.

Number of books ordered＿＿＿＿＿ @ $1.95 each ＝ $＿＿＿＿＿

Postage and Handling ＝   .25

TOTAL $＿＿＿＿＿

Name ＿＿＿＿＿＿＿＿＿＿＿＿＿＿＿＿＿＿＿＿＿＿＿＿＿＿＿＿＿

Address ＿＿＿＿＿＿＿＿＿＿＿＿＿＿＿＿＿＿＿＿＿＿＿＿＿＿＿

City ＿＿＿＿＿＿＿＿＿＿＿＿＿＿＿＿＿＿＿＿＿＿＿＿＿＿＿＿＿

State/Prov. ＿＿＿＿＿＿＿＿＿＿＿＿＿＿＿＿＿＿＿＿＿＿＿＿＿

Zip/Postal Code ＿＿＿＿＿＿＿＿＿＿＿＿＿＿＿＿＿＿＿＿＿＿＿